Patrick McDonald

Lies, LIES and APPLE PIES

THE KILLING OF THE REVEREND EDWIN ULYSSES FOXX, II

ISBN 978-1-54398-956-4 eBook 978-1-54398-957-1

PREFACE

Pleasant Valley Development Pleasant Valley, West Virginia

From a distance, the small tree looked like a bouquet of tattered yellow roses. Tall and skinny, it stood straight, as if posted like a centurion in front of the model home. Twenty feet from it, just opposite the temporary parking lot, three flags and a banner slapped to and fro in the light wind. The American flag stood tallest, while the other two advertised the logo of the builder and a banner in bright yellow with bold, blue letters that announced hopefully: *Pleasant Acres—NOW SELLING.*

The sign was wrong. They weren't selling. The new housing project of upscale homes had stalled. Kathy Ray of Valley Properties sold one the previous month, but the buyers backed out three days later after they learned of the murder in the community.

Normally, a killing in a neighborhood puts a pall over everything for a few months; but in this case, five months had passed as well as the killer being apprehended, or so the police thought. The major problem affecting real estate sales came from who had been killed, and that cast a long shadow on the situation.

Parishioners who pulled into the church parking lot one fatal Sunday morning opened their car doors to see the almost naked minister of the local Baptist church hanging half-in and half-out of a tree. The only thing between him and nature were his briefs. Across his forehead in bloody letters was the misspelled word *FORNIKATOR*. The tree remained circled in yellow police tape for at least three months after that morning. When the police tape was finally removed, the church Deacons held a meeting.

"We got to do something about that tree," Brother Tim said.

"What you got in mind?" Brother Bill asked.

"Cut it down."

"Won't do no good," Brother John interjected.

"Sure it will. People forget."

"Maybe they shouldn't."

"I'd like to bring it to a vote. All in favor of cutting it down say, 'Aye.'"

"Wait a minute," Brother Pat said. "Are we putting up a monument there or something?"

"No, no, no," Deacon Tom said. "We'll place sod over it. Grass will grow, and people will forget."

The motion passed, and grass grew, but people didn't forget.

Months later, people walked by and said, "That's where they found him. Used to be a tree there."

"He was buck naked."

Not really—he still wore his skivvies.

CHAPTER 1

(The Murder)

Thank God that November is over, thought the Reverend Edwin Ulysses Foxx, II.

The church was in a crisis; and, as the pastor, he was in the middle. Sandra, the church secretary, was openly divorcing her husband of twenty years and was secretly seeing another man. (Some rumors had it the other man was the Pastor.)

Jim Spurlock, her soon-to-be ex-husband, filed a complaint with the Board of Deacons, alleging that the pastor fired him to open the way for the affair. Adding insult to injury, the teen president of the Baptist Youth Fellowship was pregnant.

For Reverend Eddie, Saturday was normally a day of rest, a time to relax and consider last-minute changes to Sunday services. Late into the evening of December 3, 2016, he kept revising his sermon. He needed to ask the church for tolerance and kindness toward each other, especially in light of the upcoming Christmas season. Charity wasn't just giving. It also means love through understanding.

As a preacher, he needed to lead by example, or he needed to deflect the situation and contain it as the personal weaknesses of the individuals involved. Most of all, he needed to dampen the propensity of the congregation to judge others.

That was a stopgap defense. He knew tongues would be wagging again on Monday, and he'd have to fire Sandra. Then he'd have to make sure the father of April's baby married her. The church couldn't have chaos. Order was always the balm of an organization.

A church was a community within a community. Whereas the civil community had laws enforced by police, judges, and juries, the church community was normally self-policing and self-judging. In theory, the judge was the Almighty; but in Pleasant Valley, as in most places, the members wouldn't wait for the Final Judgement. They reacted like a pack of dogs ready to turn on each other at the first scent of a problem. It wasn't a Baptist problem or even a Christian one. It was a religious problem. Denominations, sects, and complete religions had been created from the judgment of a fellow believer.

The stricter the code, the narrower the way, and the easier it was to stray. Reverend Eddie knew his hands were clean. He hadn't strayed; the two women had done so. Both were close to him and under his influence. How could he stand in the pulpit on Sunday and instruct the congregation on Christian virtue when he couldn't keep his own house in order?

Church staff and youth leaders should be examples, not distractions; but they were the weak ones who fell from grace. He was inspired by the scripture verse: *We have all sinned and fallen short.* His words to use came to him clearly. His defense would be an offense, a challenge to every member to face the sin in his or her life. He would say from the pulpit that the church was going through difficult times. Of course, he would not refer to either Sandra's or April's situation. Instead, he would remind people that judgment belonged to God; and he would quote the sty-in-the-eye verse:

> *Thou hypocrite, first cast out the beam out of thine own eye and then thou shall see clearly to cast the mote out of thy brother's eye.*

Matthew 7:3-4

It was too bad Eddie was so bogged down in problems that he could not hear God's warning.

On Saturday night, December 10, at 9:25 p.m., the moon cast a silhouette like a mannequin reflecting on a dented, steel-clad security door. The faded battleship-gray door secured the church kitchen behind the recently remodeled Sunday School classroom area. The dancing shadow was the Reverend Eddie trying to insert the proper key.

His stage was a four-by-eight stoop elevated off the ground. Running late, he hurriedly pulled the door tight. A snarl of wind brought the stagnant smell of rotten food from the garbage cans lining the back wall. The lone light bulb normally illuminating the area had flickered and died one month earlier.

Reverend Eddie tried to find the keyhole in the dark. He had closed that door a thousand times; but that night, it wasn't cooperating. He pushed, but the key refused to track. He didn't know he was being watched.

Finally, the key went into the slot, and he turned the tumbler to secure the empty church. As he turned to navigate the three small steps to the ground, something whizzing past his head bounced off the steel door.

What the heck? He wondered. *Is someone throwing things at me?*

He hunkered down, trying to make his 220-pound frame smaller. "What are you doing?" he called. "No need for anger. Come out of the darkness."

A second projectile missed him by inches and stuck in the wooden door frame, vibrating. When he saw it was a hunting arrow, he ran. In the confusion, he dropped his car keys on the stoop, so he took the steps in one bound and raced toward some bushes.

Car lights came on, blinding him. The car accelerated toward him. He froze, then jumped to the right at the last second. The left front of the car smashed into his left leg in a glancing blow, knocking him into the thorny wild rose bush.

He tried to roll even deeper into the bushes, but the stiff, backward thorns of the bush cut into his flesh. The stems, as thick as his finger, fanned out into a network of thorns resembling half-inch shark fins. The living concertina wire created an impenetrable barrier. He curled into a fetal position and started praying and whimpering.

The car stopped, and the driver opened the door. Reverend Eddie recognized him and thought there might be a chance to reason with him.

"Please, I'm sorry. She was a mistake. I meant you no harm."

The pursuer got out and retrieved his bow from the front seat, then he reached into his quiver for another arrow. Reverend Eddie remained balled up like a possum.

"Yes," his enemy said. "She was YOUR mistake. God sent me to punish you." His voice was calm and even.

"I didn't mean it. You have to understand that the flesh is weak." He curled up even tighter. "God has forgiven me," the Rev. continued. "Can you?"

"God has not forgiven you. I am here for Him. He sent me."

Reverend Eddie jumped to his feet and attacked the man. The bow fell to one side, and the arrow dropped between them. Both grabbed for it, but the attacker reached it first. Taking it in two hands, he thrust it upward and through the preacher's heart.

CHAPTER 2

(The Discovery)

The next morning, the crisp air was thick with moisture. A few more degrees colder, and it would snow. Frank Hawkins pulled his gray Ford Focus into the church parking lot at 8:08 a.m. A few minutes early, he wanted to practice his solo before anyone arrived.

Getting out of his car, he slid the key into the slot to lock it when he looked up and saw a foot hanging down through some branches. His gaze traveled upward until he saw it was a man, nearly naked, his chin resting against his chest. At first, the choir director thought it was a mannequin, then he saw the blood directly under the figure.

"My God! It's the preacher!"

The police and the village ambulance arrived within fifteen minutes. Sergeant Scott Adkins, the on-duty officer when the call came in, pulled up first in his dark blue Ford Victoria. As he stepped out of his squad car, he saw the preacher's naked leg dangling in midair.

"Damn," he muttered. "He's hanging like a *piñata*."

Sergeant Adkins' superior, Chief Robert Bentley, led the small police force and was out of town for his birthday. He and his wife, Dorothy, were at Hilton Head, North Carolina, enjoying themselves at a condo owned by a friend. As the Chief of Police of a small town, he enjoyed a modest salary, a decent health plan, a livable retirement program, and, best of all, the ability to escape for a few days at a time when he had the mood. Crime in Pleasant Valley was like sex at a convent—seldom and modest.

Bentley's cell phone's chirping ring was loud, sharp, and annoying. The caller ID revealed the special number for Sergeant Adkins, the officer in charge while Bentley was away.

"Chief, you've got to come back," Sergeant Adkins said. "We've had a murder. Reverend Eddie's dead."

"What?" Chief Bentley adjusted the phone in his hand. "The Reverend? What happened?"

"Don't know yet. He's hanging by rope in the church's tree in his skivvies. We're getting the volunteer fire department out to bring him down."

"When did it happen?"

The sergeant paused, considering. "Sometime last night. He was discovered about an hour ago, around eight o'clock."

"When did you get the call?"

"About ten minutes after eight."

"And why did it take you an hour to call me?"

"I didn't believe it at first. Then I wanted to see it with my own eyes. I didn't want to bother you until it was verified."

"OK. I understand. Call off the volunteers. They could screw up the crime scene. I'll be there in two hours, assuming I can get a charter at the Hilton Head Island Airport. Secure the area and leave him in the tree."

"Sir, this has spread like wildfire. At first, there were a few lookers, then church members arrived for services, and now we've got about two hundred gawkers. Someone called the TV station. I don't know if I can wait two or three hours to take him down."

"Make busy. Extend the police line; situate the hook and ladder truck to block the view. No one touches that body until I'm back."

"Sir, I'll do my best. He's naked up there, and the killer cut off his fingers."

Feeling frustrated but calm, the Chief said, "Scott, just rope it off and extend the crime scene. Make sure no one touches that body until I get there. I'll be in touch in twenty minutes to let you know which local airport I'm using. Have a cruiser waiting."

"Yes Sir."

The Chief, hanging up, scratched his chin nervously. Who would want to kill such an obnoxious do-gooder?

"Dorothy, Honey," he said. "We've got a problem, an emergency back home. It's not our kids. It's work-related. The Reverend Eddie Foxx done got himself killed. I must go back right now. I have to go to the island airport and see if I can get a charter to Huntington or Charleston."

His wife sat on the bed with one hand pressed against her mouth. "Who'd want to kill Reverend Eddie?"

"A whole lot of people. That's what I have to find out."

She knew he was duty bound and nodded. "You go. I understand. If necessary, I can drive back later today. Why did he have to get himself killed on your birthday?"

"Don't know, but you'll have to drive me to the airport next to the National Wildlife Refuge. It's big enough that I should be able to find a charter. It's a damn shame this is Sunday. That'll make it harder."

Dorothy drove him the eight miles to the little airport on the far northeastern part of the island. As she pulled up to the civil aviation area, she asked, "Want me to wait in case you have to go to Savannah to get out of here?"

"Good idea. Just double park here. If anyone hassles you, tell them it's a police emergency. I'll call from the charter area and let you know if I have a plane." He leaned over for a good-bye kiss that was a little more passionate than usual.

Her cell phone rang less than ten minutes later. "I'll be in Pleasant Valley in about two hours. You wouldn't believe what this will cost. I used the Village's credit card. I hope they have a high limit. There goes our bonus for the year."

It was five hundred and thirty-two miles direct, but the King Air 100 couldn't take that route. At a top speed of 296 mph, It circled around Charlotte because of the hub traffic from commercial airlines. (The King usually cruised at 270 mph). The Chief called Scott from the plane to make sure Corporal Jenkins would be waiting to pick him up at the Ona Airpark, west of Milton, at 11:45 a.m.

The trip was uneventful until they arrived. The twin UACL Pratt & Whitney PT6A.28 reverse-flow free-spool turboprop engines performed to specifications. At first the pilot lined up with the runway, then he did a fly-by, muttering into his mike as if saying a Hail Mary.

The runway was charted at 3,154 feet, and the King Air needed almost all of that, normally landing in 2,700 feet, but there was a tricky crosswind and that 400-foot safety margin would be eaten up in less than three seconds.

The pilot, making a large, sweeping turn, leveled out at eighty feet above the valley floor, aimed at the runway. The wheels touched down at 300 feet with a screech of rubber hitting cement. In two seconds, the pilot reversed engines. With a roar and a jerk, the plane ground to a halt 225 feet short of the runway's end at 11:48 a.m.

With a smile, the pilot turned toward the small building that served as airport headquarters and taxied closer. The Chief, his stomach in his throat, deplaned and headed for the Village's police car parked nearby with its lights blinking red and blue.

He nodded to the pilot. "Great job." He ran toward the car at two hours and eighteen minutes since Sergeant Adkins' call.

Feeling the vehicle's four wheels on the ground, accompanied by the flashing lights and siren wail, helped the Chief relax. He would be back in Pleasant Valley in twenty minutes and hoped the men had waited.

The streets of the village were deserted. There was no traffic until they turned the corner to Jackie Lane, where a crowd stretched for a quarter mile. Cars were parked randomly, and people milled in large groups like flocks of crows picking a harvested cornfield.

Corporal Jenkins, nosing the cruiser ahead through the throng, drove as necessary on the sidewalk, street, and grass to reach the church.

At two hundred yards from the crime scene, the crowd thinned out, and a barrier of yellow crime-scene tape separated the regular citizens from the civil servants.

Chief Bentley and Corporal Jenkins stopped forty feet from the tree. A cherry picker was directly in front of it, obscuring their view, while a photographer stood in the basket, taking pictures.

"Who's that?" the Chief asked as he jumped out of the patrol car.

Sergeant Adkins answered just a little hesitantly. "Well, Chief, that's Frank Ramey of the *Herald Dispatch*."

"Who said he could take those pictures? We don't want the preacher with his dick hanging out on the front page of the *Dispatch*."

"It's not that, Sir. You said to stall, and I did my best. His camera's better than ours. He volunteered to take the crime-scene photos and promised us first pick."

"Did he promise not to print them in the paper?"

"He's a good guy. He won't cross me. He said we could have the first ones. Besides, you weren't here."

Chief Bentley surveyed the crowd and crime scene. "What a mess. This is a management failure, and I'm the manager. Thank you for leaving him in the tree. Job well done. After I have a closer observation, get him down and keep this area secure.

The sudden interruption of his vacation and the quick flight back to West Virginia with its messy crime scene almost overwhelmed him. He needed to call his wife and tell her about the situation. Most of all, he needed a hot meal and strong cup of coffee. But first, the crime scene awaited his walk through. Then he would head for The Mug and the hard bench that was his special seat.

CHAPTER 3

(The Headline)

Above the fold, in the Monday morning *Herald Dispatch*, was printed a picture of the pastor in the tree in his underpants. The editor chose to X out his manly area, adding about twenty-five percent more X's than needed. Apparently, the story wasn't big enough already:

MINISTER MURDERED

PLEASANT VALLEY NOT SO PLEASANT

It wasn't usual to find Chief Bentley's door closed. Sergeant Adkins tapped tepidly.

"Come in!"

Walking in, he saw the Chief staring at photos of the crime scene on his desk.

"Sir, I'm sorry about the story in the *Herald Dispatch*." He held his hat in his hand. "I trusted him."

"Not your fault. You're a trusting man. I asked you to stall; and, for the most part, you did. It was a testing time. I appreciate your good work. I was just reviewing our set of the photos. Ramey took some good ones. They might be helpful in the long run."

"Thank you, Sir. One more thing."

"Yes?"

"I'd like to be the officer in charge of the crime scene."

"I don't know. I need you here. We'll be getting a lot of calls, and I need you to screen them."

"You're the Chief, but Jenkins can do it. I'm the most-experienced officer. I qualified third in my class at the State Police crime school last summer."

"If I remember correctly, that class had only five or six."

"Not the point, Sir. We all did well. I have the experience, and I'm requesting the opportunity."

The Chief mulled it over for a second. "Request granted. Get Jenkins in here and keep me apprised of your findings."

Late in the day, Chief Bentley expanded the perimeter around the tree and borrowed some deputies from the Cabell County Sheriff's Department to further secure the area until it could be harvested.

Unfortunately, the crime scene was strewn with garbage. The tech team, wearing rubber gloves, retrieved cans, bottles, boxes, paper tablecloths, and debris that came from an alternative party held by the church's youth group who didn't want to attend the high school dance after the football game.

All evidence had to be photographed, mapped, and catalogued before it was removed from the area.

The blood evidence took priority. The largest pool of blood was on and under a multiflora rose bush. The thorny, branched shrub, which had quarter-sized pink and white roses during the first chill of September, now had only the Rev.'s blood. A blended color of black and red dripped from the stems when a rubber-gloved hand reached for it. Blood had also soaked onto the ropes that had secured the pastor to his heavenly perch. And then there were the ten small splotches of blood in two patches of five: they formed two semicircles on the sidewalk leading from the church's kitchen.

"This must be where the killer cut off Foxx's fingers," a crime-lab tech said. "Photograph, photograph before we collect. All will be analyzed."

The team also found a bloody sock, but they didn't know which foot it came from or what happened to the rest of the pastor's clothes.

In addition to blood, ropes, and garbage, they found the keys to the church, a flat square-head nail, and tiny splinters of orange-amber Plexiglas. The grass adjacent to the asphalt parking lot had multiple ruts and tire marks, because it was used as excess parking for church activities. The team decided to skip taking tire-print molds, because all the members had recently parked there. It would mean weak evidence in court and too many leads to follow.

Back at the office, the Chief held up the plastic bag containing the square, flat nail. "Haven't seen one of these in a long time. It's an old-fashioned horse nail. If we don't tie this to the crime, the defense attorney will claim the headless horseman did it."

In addition to the physical evidence collected, there was the body and the resulting autopsy. The body was now in the Cabell County Morgue for autopsy by the county pathologist. The conclusion was death by arrow, though the report also noted his left leg was fractured. He had a large bruise on his upper torso, indicating he'd been hit by a car.

Forty-two-year old James Alan, M.D., was young to be the Cabell County coroner; but, sadly, he had plenty of experience with homicides.

Shooting victims, knife assaults, asphyxiations and a few heart-wrenching child victims. However, this was his first bow-and-arrow case.

After a close exam, he ruled out the bow and declared that death was caused by an arrow that had been stabbed into the deceased's heart:

> "It is my conclusion that the killer stabbed the victim with the arrow in an upward thrust, severing the aorta. The digits were cut off crudely with a dull instrument."

The next few days were a flurry of activity. Even though the Chief initially ruled out the tire prints, because that would mean every member of the congregation would be a suspect, he decided they had to be taken. The bloody patch by the rose bush was photographed, measured, and had soil samples carried off in plastic bags.

CHAPTER 4

(The Fist of God)

Two days after the discovery of the body, a letter arrived at the Pleasant Valley Police Deprtment:

> "I killed him, and I'm not sorry. He had to die. He did things that signed his fate. It was God's will, not mine. If I told you the things he did, you would know who I am. One thing I'm not is a fool. You would have killed him, too. Let it rest. The Fist of God"

The letter arrived in a plain white envelope. It was written on lined paper from a spiral notebook and was addressed to the Chief. The stamp was a heart with *LOVE* on it.

Holding the letter carefully by the edges, the Chief slipped it into a plastic Ziploc bag. "There might be DNA or fingerprints on this. He may have licked the stamp. I want this to go to the state lab in Charleston. Drive it up there this afternoon and tell them to put a rush on it. We have a killer in our midst."

He spoke without looking up, knowing that Sergeant Adkins was within earshot and observing him. He was like a fly on the wall, always present, always flitting in and out, and often in the way. A trip to Charleston would at least occupy him elsewhere for the rest of the day.

Chief Bentley took out a sheet of paper and drew a line down the center from top to bottom. One column was labeled *Male,* the other *Female.* Under the word *Female,* he wrote the word *Sex.*

He thought about the letter, wondering: *Did the writer mean Rev. Eddie did things to himself or did he mean Rev. Eddie did things to others or did he mean Rev. Eddie just did things?*

The Chief's main question was: *What devil chased the Reverend up that tree?* After thinking about it for a minute, he studied the list, wondering which column to use to fit the sin. Lust was definitely on the male side. Gluttony didn't seem applicable. Wrath could go either way. Envy? Would someone kill over that? Pride was another weak reason to kill. Wrath and revenge were good motives, but they were gender neutral.

The signature of *The Fist of God* certainly sounded manly. The letter was mailed from Huntington, which is only eighteen miles from Pleasant Valley.

CHAPTER 5

(The Funeral)

Five days after the murder, the church's parking lot was full. Cars even parked on the grass, some near trees with yellow tape.

The funeral of the Reverend Edwin Foxx drew an ecumenical crowd, most of which were Baptist. Could it be that everyone in town was at the church. Two old folks and the nurse from an assisted living facility were not there. And Sam, the butcher, was in a Huntington hospital recovering from complications after having a pacemaker inserted in his chest.

The Methodist minister and forty of his flock sat in the middle section in a bloc, as if they were at a political convention, *sans* placards. The eighteen Catholics also sat as a unit, as did the six Jews. Even the town's two professed atheists came, although they didn't sit together.

Widow Foxx sat in the front row, the seat she normally occupied when she silently critiqued Reverend Eddie's sermons. She wore a simple black dress with three-quarter sleeves, a high neckline, and a hem just below her knees. Her head, face, and neck were adorned with a stiff, black veil that resembled medieval chain mail, thick, black, and impenetrable. She looked like the love child of Joan of Arc and Darth Vader.

The packed church required metal folding chairs to accommodate the overflow. Murmuring voices hushed as the Baptist minister on loan from the Fifth Avenue Baptist Church of Huntington stood and walked to the podium.

"Ladies and Gentlemen, a moment of prayer," he said. "Beloved, we come together today to celebrate the life of Edwin Foxx. He is Your child, Father, an appointed shepherd, who for the past nine years blessed Pleasant Valley with his leadership, counsel, and love. He will be missed, but we take comfort in knowing that he is now with You. He will live forever in Your bosom, will walk the golden streets of Heaven, and will sing with the heavenly choir.

"We thank You, our Father, Who made us and Who supplies our every need, Who loves us and sustains us. We ask not why but rather that Your will be done. In Jesus' name we pray. Amen."

In death, Reverend Foxx was bigger than in life. He would have been proud to have officiated over such a large funeral, but instead, he was the guest of honor, a dubious role. Most of the crowd came to mourn, though others were there to gawk and say, "I was there."

The ceremony was formal and pompous for a rural church, as if the deceased were the Pope of Paducah or the Arch Bishop of Cabell instead of a simple Baptist minister. Most funerals are edited events, where the bad is erased, and the good is amplified. This one proved no different.

The church was decorated with mostly black banners, an odd combination of celebration and the macabre. The Widow Foxx requested it, saying, "Nothing is too good for Eddie."

The casket was made of deeply polished walnut of the finest quality. The Reverend's head and upper body were displayed down to his waist, his fingerless hands tucked under the drape. The suit was a new one sold by the funeral home to the widow.

"You can't have him heading to heaven in old clothes," the funeral director said.

It was silk with a new, formal white shirt and expensive cufflinks. She wanted nothing but the best for Eddie.

The church paid for the cost of the funeral, one of the clauses in his employment contract.

His eyes were closed as if he were in prayer. His stoic, pondering expression made him seem as if he contemplated the mysteries of the universe. In the fifth row, a pensive Chief of Police sat, his mind on the mystery of what trouble caused Reverend Eddie's death. More importantly, who killed him?

The Chief surveyed the room, knowing the killer was probably there. It was a crime of passion and hate; yet, as he studied the faces around him that morning, he saw only boredom or apathy. One of them did it, though. There was a killer in the room.

CHAPTER 6

(The Barber)

One of the last-minute attendees was Ray-Bob Raymond, the town barber. He silently found a folding chair at the end of the last row and sat down during the opening prayer. It was his first church appearance in many years.

He debated coming, but the town was pretty much shut down for the funeral, and he feared his absence might be conspicuous. The most important reason for his attendance was Sandra, who would be there with her soon-to-be ex-husband. Ray-Bob donned his only tie and reluctantly attended. From his standing position at the back of the fully occupied building, all he could see was the back of the other attendees' heads, a comforting sight.

After the final Amen, the Widow Foxx and visiting family members were escorted out. The usher emptied the church row-by-row beginning at the front. Ray-Bob considered stepping out without waiting for the parade of attendees, but he felt it was necessary to let everyone see him there. He also wanted to see the body language and disposition of Jim and Sandra Spurlock, as they walked by.

He left the church with a heavy heart, wondering what he had done. When Sandy walked past, escorted by her husband, she didn't make eye contact. Jim, on the other hand, looked him squarely in the eye, smirking.

Sandy told Ray-Bob she had to attend with her husband for appearance's sake. The way they walked out together, though, made it look as if they had just walked down the aisle in a wedding ceremony. For Ray-Bob, that took the *fun* out of *funeral*.

Ray-Bob's observation of Sandra and Jim was mostly correct. She called him the next day.

"Got a minute to talk?" she asked.

"Sure."

"I don't know where to start. I think we need to step back. There. I said it. You're important to me, but so is Jim. After the funeral, we got to talking, and, well, we need time before we end our marriage. I invested eighteen years in that man, and he isn't that bad. Part of the problem is me. I guess I wanted more, to be a princess and have a rainbow, but I couldn't stand the rain. Jim's a good man. He's peculiar, as we all are in our own way.

"Anyhow, he still loves me, and I still have feelings for him. It wouldn't be fair to you to be with you under false pretenses. You won't hate me, will you?"

At the time, Ray-Bob sat in his barber chair, staring at his reflection across the room, seeing multiple images of himself bounce between the mirrors on both sides of the room in a chain of diminishing reflections. Her words cut to his heart, and he felt deflated. She'd been the one shining moment in his otherwise lonely life. Somehow, the transcendental solitude of his respite to the Mud River cabin would never replace the moments he gazed at her across the tabletop in a corner booth at Rebels and Redcoats. Of course, there was the sex, too.

"Sandy, I'll never hate you." He wanted to say more, but he didn't want her to hear the quiver in his voice. "Take care, Honey. Take care." He hung up.

Standing, he walked to the door, flipped the sign to read *Closed*, locked the door, and headed for his car. The tremor in his hands made him unfit to trim anyone's hair that day.

CHAPTER 7

(The P.V. Police Dept.)

Pleasant Valley was proud of its low crime rate and the efficiency of its village police force. A murder changed that overnight. Without any clues and the story getting only brief reports by the Huntington and Charleston newspapers, a mixture of fear and embarrassment spread throughout the town.

The Pleasant Valley Police Department with its three officers (including the Chief) and an occasional receptionist was housed in a 980-square foot annex built as an extension of the Village Town Hall. An afterthought, it had been added ten years after the Hall was completed. The rooflines didn't match, and the slightly different tone of the brown roof tiles set the Police Department apart even though it was part of the building. The entryway led to a reception room and then a secured area on the other side of a Dutch door.

The area looked like something designed for a veterinarian's office, with a sign that read, *Dogs on this side, cats down here, and everything else take a seat by the door.*

Once buzzed through to the secure side, a visitor met a maze of small hallways leading to a few small rooms. Two were holding cells, and two were small offices equipped with desks and computers where officers wrote out their reports and took naps. A small kitchen area was adjacent to a unisex bathroom with one seat, one urinal, and one basin.

On the other side of the wall from the john was the Chief's large office, which doubled as a conference room when necessary.

The Village budget was tight, and the holding cells, kitchen, and bathroom were placed so only one set of plumbing lines and one sewer line were needed along the back wall. Although there was a reception area, there was no money for fulltime help, so the small desk on the other side of the reception window was manned by Sergeant Adkins during the day and closed at night.

The village grew by over 1,000 residences since the annex was built, but the force remained the same. There was no need to add another one, and there was no room to house him, anyway.

CHAPTER 8

(The Fist of God)

In the morning mail, a letter in a beige envelope came to Sergeant Adkins' attention. It bore a *LOVE* stamp like the first, and it was also addressed to Chief Bentley. Sergeant Adkins, holding it by the edges, gently placed it on the Chief's desk.

"Got another letter," he announced. "Maybe this time it'll be a confession."

The first letter went through all the tests possible at the Charleston State Crime Lab and came back without any DNA. The stamp was self-sticking, so there was no saliva, and it held no fingerprints. The killer was clever, but such people always made a mistake.

The Chief gingerly opened the new letter:

"Bentley,

I asked you to leave it alone. I explained it had to be done. You sit in your swivel chair and judge me. I did your job. I took a horrendous, depraved person off our streets. Keep it up, and this will come home to roost. Give it a rest, a long one. You don't want to find me.

The Fist of God"

Chief Bentley, lowering his reading glasses, contemplated the letter. The only time he heard Reverend Eddie preach was about a letter Paul wrote to the Galatians. It seemed as if the Reverend examined every word, explaining that a word prescribed by God held deeper meaning that those given it by man.

He challenged the church to read with an eye toward God, and not just read the words but to seek their meaning. Paul was the messenger who tried to tell the Galatians something, though what that was, Reverend Eddie never said.

The Chief pondered for a moment. Maybe the Fist of God held a deeper meaning than the words on the page. He read the letter a second time and didn't like what he saw.

With the swivel chair reference, the killer showed he'd been in the Chief's office. The words *our streets* meant it was a local. The murderer was one of them, someone who'd been in his office.

The final line, though, gave him the most concern: *this will come home to roost.*

If the killer was trying to get the Chief to back off, it was a misdirected attempt. The Chief was becoming obsessed with finding out who killed the preacher. The reason no longer mattered. The method was known, so who became the primary question. The Chief pledged to himself that the person who wrapped his deeds in the vengeance of God would be brought to justice.

"Adkins!" he shouted. When no one answered, he muttered, "Why is he never here when I need him and always here when I want to be alone?"

A small voice came from the restroom door. "Be there in a moment."

Thirty seconds later, Sergeant Adkins emerged shaking his dripping hands. "Yes, Sir. You want something?"

"Yeah. How long ago did we get this swivel chair?"

"I don't know. Maybe six or seven months ago."

"I need a list of everyone who's been in my office in the past seven months."

"Sir, I don't think I can do that. I've got a good memory, but it ain't photographic. We don't keep a log, but I'll try. Maybe your day sheets will be a start."

"Good idea. I'll start there. By the way, who cleans the place? Have we had any service work done in the past seven months? Who delivered the chair?"

The Chief had a rabbit trail, and he intended to find the rabbit before he looked like Alice in Wonderland.

CHAPTER 9

(Pre-Murder, Rev. Eddie)

To understand the who, why, and why nots of the killing of the Reverend Eddie, one must step back in time and live in the victim's shoes. Perhaps *victim* is too strong a word. *Deceased* might be the better choice.

A village is like a quilt, one block after another sewed together by threads. Viewing one section in isolation may cause distortion of the whole. The Reverend was part of all he met. The village was a conglomeration of families, singles, straights, and homosexuals. There was a smidgen of authenticity, a diversity of political opinion; but, basically, the village of Pleasant Valley was a white cotton quilt with splashes of color here and there as an accent.

The census showed a predominantly white protestant community of middle-aged people, mostly married with 2.54 children. The homes and infrastructure of the village were younger than surrounding towns. The community was more affluent than those areas, too. Pleasant Valley was a very nice place to live.

It looked like a Swiss village as downsized by Disney. The surrounding hills were pretty and rolling, not steep and majestic. It wasn't one valley but a series of them with undulating hills. The village boundaries stretched from Fudges Creek Road (County Road 29) on the east side, to 1,000 feet west of Tom's Creek Road (County Road 31) at the point where the Guyandotte River made an oxbow turn around Esquire Golf Course. The south side ended at Cavil Creek Road, and the north end followed Clark Hollow Road until it petered out and followed an imaginary line to Burk Hollow.

A series of streams, mostly intermittent creeks, flowed into either the Mud River or the Guyandotte River. The hillsides were rich in geologic rock outcroppings that held fern fossils from the Pennsylvanian Age. The hills, green with trees, were filled with squirrels, possums, raccoons, and deer.

The one thousand acres once belonged to the Yeager family before they moved to the Hamlin area a few miles away. For years, Pleasant Valley supplied natural gas to the larger cities of Huntington and Charleston. A few active gas wells produced small dividends for their investors. The timber on the hills traced its roots to the primeval forest of the Devonian Period. Most of the forest had been cut and milled to become barn poles or roof rafters. Some formed the foundations of hillside homes, while others became the roof supports for mines or railroad ties for the southwest portion of West Virginia.

The village was designed by a real-estate developer who secured the land in the late 1990's. The village center was six blocks square, with streets running out like spokes from the center of a wagon wheel. None of the streets were straight for more than a few hundred yards before they turned to accommodate the small valleys, twisting around until they almost returned to their starting point.

The name Pleasant Valley was very appropriate, since it was an ideal place to live. Positioned between Huntington and Charleston, the Huntington Mall was closer to Pleasant Valley than it was to most of Huntington. An hour's drive east led to Charleston, the state capital.

It wasn't a hick town. It was prosperous and harmonious. Reverend Eddie felt privileged to be, in his mind, the religious center of such a town.

To understand the man's death, one must know the man, but that wasn't easy, because he didn't know himself. Eddie Foxx was the oldest of three, the only boy in his family. His parents were teachers in the Logan County School System. They had met at Marshall University, a great school for West Virginia educators.

Both felt a commitment to education and to work toward bettering their community. Although two years apart and living within two hollows of each other in Mingo County, they didn't meet until a perfect spring day in 1972. Within five years, they had three children.

Edwin, the oldest, was named after an uncle who was a chaplain in Viet Nam and who died in the Tet Offensive during the Battle of Hue. Uncle Ed refused to leave the wounded soldiers when the North Vietnamese overran the small hospital in Hue-Phu Bai. The Foxx family held hope he was captured, but they later learned he'd been killed while praying over a fallen soldier.

The name and legend became a legacy for Edwin Foxx, and he took them seriously. To be as good as Uncle Ed was his primary ambition until at age fifteen, when he had an epiphany. *Why shouldn't I be better?* He asked himself. *Did Adam sin because of Eve? No. It was because he said, "Yes," when offered an apple. Adam agreed to sin. Is it not possible to be better than Adam, better than Peter and Paul, each of whom came up short during trying times? I could even be a better man than Uncle Ed.*

Plotting out his life's path, Rev. Eddie felt in control. He knew that choice, not providence, set man's destiny. He would choose correctly, always taking right over wrong, wholesomeness over worldliness.

By that decision, the fifteen-year-old's skinny shoulders squared and accepted the burden of choice. Like all other teenagers, he faced choices every day, but he vowed to think, ponder, consider, reflect, and, if necessary, consult with God. The result would be order, not chaos—or so his theory went.

He knew perfection wasn't possible, but the pursuit of perfection would be his guide. Like a navigator fixed on the North Star without trying to reach it, Edwin would follow his own beacon during his life. He would take the straight path, heedless of circumstances or barriers thrown up by society. In his mind and in his actions, he would be above such things.

The following Sunday, the minister's message struck close to young Edwin's thoughts. The sermon was on pride. *Pride goes before destruction, a haughty spirit before a fall.* [Proverbs 16:18]

Although it troubled Eddie that pride was considered a sin, he was proud of the fact he was better than other people. They sinned, but he restrained himself. Why shouldn't he be proud? If pride was a sin, he reasoned, it had to be a small one.

That thought sent his mind into emotional spasms. Was a small sin not a sin? Was eating the apple a small sin? Who decided the severity of the sin? He had so many questions, but there were no answers.

He realized it was a test from God. The answers were in the Bible. It took an interpretation by a Biblical scholar to find the answers and explain them to the laity. God was clearly calling him to be that person.

His pride wasn't too great after all. He was just pleased with himself, not prideful or boastful. Being pleased wasn't a sin. God was calling him to be a leader who could decipher the truth for the uninformed or unenlightened.

Eddie's high school was a ruthless test in the game of survival, but he tried. Holding to his principals, he had few friends, only one date, and was always the odd man out. He wore his oddness like a badge of courage. Others, he knew, were weak, but he was strong. Others sinned, but he withheld, withdrew, and withstood the test. Every day, the world tried to up the ante and make his path steeper, the road more slippery, and his direction a hog's trough of mud.

When Edwin Foxx graduated high school, he was relieved. He was headed for a Christian college. Even better, it was a Baptist college where he hoped to meet like-minded, dedicated young people. His church offered him a partial scholarship to Alderson Broaddus, a liberal arts school in Philippi, West Virginia, a small town of 2,500 people, where he majored in Christian Studies and minored in Communications.

The college was a combination of two schools, each named for a distinguished Baptist leader. The Broaddus was named after Reverend William Francis Ferguson Broaddus, a prominent minister at the time of the Civil War, and the Alderson was named for a committed Baptist laywoman named Emma Cornelia Alderson. Though their names were linked, they never met. He was fifty-nine when she was born, and he'd been dead sixty-six years when she died in 1942.

The college sat on some high ground called Battle Hill, overlooking the Tygart River Valley. Philippi's claim to fame, other than being the most-misspelled town in America, was for being the scene of the first land battle of the Civil War and the place where a young general named George B. McClellan made his name. His three thousand troops made an overnight forced march through a downpour of rain and thunderstorms and overwhelmed eight hundred poorly equipped Confederate troops. The Confederates ran so fast that the battle was named the Philippi Races and was reenacted each June as part of the Blue-Gray reunion.

For Edwin Foxx, it was a 190-mile, four-hour road trip across West Virginia from Logan to Philippi. More than the distance, he felt a sense of freedom. His burdens were lifted for the first time in his life, because in Philippi there were other people like him. He was no longer alone in his thinking.

The school's motto is *You can do that here.* He felt liberated, still bound by his standards of perfection but in an atmosphere where perfection was an attribute, not a cross to bear.

As classes commenced and three years rolled by, he excelled in his studies. But one day in the Pickett Library, something different happened to his routine. It was the fall of 2000, and he was a senior. There may have been some divine inspiration when the young lady sitting across from him at a large table in the reference section spilled her purse while looking for a pen. The pen made a fast roll to land in Eddie's lap. Her eyes followed the path but quickly averted when the pen left the side of the table and landed in his nether regions.

He immediately retrieved it and handed it back with a smile. She smiled and mouthed, "Thank you. Sorry."

Within a few minutes, they were talking. Half an hour later, they were at the Hamer Center student union, enjoying lunch together.

She was a nursing major who wanted to become a missionary. She was radiant, and he was enamored and enraptured, completely smitten. To him, that had to be what love was, a perfect helpmate. She would be everything he needed in a minister's wife. For six weeks, they dined together, took walks, talked, and planned. A new horizon filled with possibilities waiting in their future.

Then one night in early December, their passions took flight, and they lived up to the school motto, "You can do that here." And they did.

Edwin immediately knew it was a mistake. His plan was to save himself for marriage. Now, he was no longer pure and had failed a test in life. When he was offered a bite of the forbidden apple, he took it. The devil used this girl as Eve to seduce him and show him he was just a man. For every Samson there was a Delilah, for every David a Bathsheba. For Edwin Foxx, there was Emma.

He avoided his forbidden apple the following day and the day after. Finally, she caught up with him, as he walked to a class. Seeing her, he walked faster, but she picked up her pace to confront him.

"Eddie, what's wrong? You seem distant and angry."

He stopped and moved his face very close to hers. "Angry, no. Disappointed, yes. You robbed me, took the special walk I had with God from me. You pushed me from the garden and are of the devil. Please, never speak to me again. Don't walk the same path as I. For you, it was nothing. For me, it was an end. Now, I must start a new beginning." With that odd comment, he walked out of her life and avoided women as if they were rabid dogs.

After graduating from Alderson Broaddus, the newly appointed Reverend Eddie Foxx spent some time as a youth pastor for South Charleston Baptist. There he met Beverly, the daughter of the deacon widower who chaired the search committee and who was secretly looking for a husband for one of his three girls.

Beverly, the oldest, was twenty-four, while the youngest was nineteen. There was little harmony in their home. Deacon Lusk lost his wife four years earlier and immediately gained three young women who wanted to tell him what to do or not do.

"Dad, you should wait five years to date again," one said.

It wasn't just his social life they controlled, but all aspects of every day. The ringleader was Beverly.

A few months after Eddie had his initial interview, there was a wedding at the church and a reception in the fellowship hall for the four hundred guests. Foxx had met his mate, and she was carnivorous.

Beverly was ambitious for her husband. Why should his talent be hidden in his role as youth pastor? He needed a pulpit.

The search began; and, in the summer of 2006, when Edwin Foxx first preached from the pulpit of Pleasant Valley Baptist Church, he knew that he'd come home. This was his calling. He would grow this rural church to become a leader in the region, then the state.

Beverly had a different kind of growth in mind. She wanted to start a family, but try as they had, nothing resulted. With fourteen-hour days, endless committees and programs, visitations, marriages to perform, funerals to preside over, and hospitals to visit, Reverend Eddie was too tired to have sex.

Beverly spent time with Internet searches, books on fertility and infertility, and visits to her OB/GYN in Huntington. Dr. Gilbert, after appropriate tests, assured her that her reproductive organs were fine, and her chemistry was in good balance.

"You probably need to wait and relax. Let nature take its course. Sometimes, you want too much and try too hard. Give it six months, and things will probably be all right. If not, you may wish to have your husband tested."

"Why not test him right now?" she asked with determination that wouldn't be denied.

"We could arrange it, but most men are sensitive when it comes to questions of fertility. They take it as an attack on their manliness."

"Oh, I can handle that," she said with a knowing smile.

That evening, Reverend Eddie opened the front door of his four-bedroom room and was surprised to smell beef cooking. Apparently, they were having hamburgers that evening. He walked down the narrow hall and saw the dining room table set with a starched white tablecloth, fine china, and crystal goblets.

"Beverly, are we having guests tonight?"

"No, just the two of us."

"In the dining room?"

"I thought it would be a nice change." She pulled steaks from the broiler.

Within a few minutes, she assembled a large tossed salad, hot rolls, twice-baked potatoes, and two prime tenderloins. Reverend Eddie almost said something but decided to wait and let her tell him when she was ready.

He pulled out a chair to seat her, then sat beside her and took her hand. "It's time to thank the Lord for this bounty."

He offered a new prayer appropriate for the moment, whatever that might be. As he said, "Amen," he almost asked, "To what do we owe this?" But good sense prevailed, so he chewed his steak.

With a smile, he began the standard small talk for a ten-plus year marriage. "The food is great. Thank you for your efforts. How did your day go?" He wiped his mouth with his napkin, refusing to be drawn into whatever she planned.

"I hope your day went well." She added the dreaded words, "There are things we need to talk about."

The steak in his stomach hunkered down as if seeking shelter. His breathing accelerated, and his pulse increased. "I thought this was unusual. I hope it's a good thing. Apparently, it's important enough for you to go to the trouble of preparing this dinner." He immediately wished he hadn't used the word *trouble,* but it was too late.

"No trouble. I wanted you to give me your full attention—no church stuff or local politics. It's just you and me over a simple dinner, wife to husband."

Shuddering slightly, he stopped himself from reaching for his water glass, realizing his hand was shaking. Sloshing water wasn't the kind of signal he wanted to send. He calmly folded his hands, his fingers interlaced, and said, "You have my full attention."

Beverly leaned forward in her chair. "I don't think we're trying hard enough."

"Trying what hard enough?"

"I'll be thirty-four next month. My mother had three children by age twenty-five."

Oh, no, he thought, *not this again. At least she isn't saying I'm putting the church ahead of our marriage.* "Honey, if God wants us to have children, we will. Sarah in the Bible...."

"I'm not Sarah, and I won't wait until I'm ninety to conceive. We need to do this now. I want you to see the doctor and be tested for fertility. Maybe they're anemic. Maybe when you sit all day, they get too hot and die. Whatever it is, the doctor can help us."

He paused for several seconds, bit his tongue, then spoke. "No doctor. I'll take vitamin E. I'll walk around the office more. I'll change to boxers, not briefs, but no doctor."

"Eddie, I'm asking you. Please do this for me. Do it for us."

"I can't. You don't know what you're asking. When I go for my physical, they give me a cup, and I know what to do. I fill it with pee. When *this* doctor hands me a cup, he isn't looking for pee. Two of the nurses at the clinic go to our church. There's no way I'll fill that cup. Besides, I don't think I'm shooting blanks."

Beverly slowly sat back in her chair. Reaching into her lap, she gently and deliberately folded her napkin and set it on the table, then she stood and walked from the room without a word.

The steak in his stomach felt like it was tying itself in knots.

Beverly didn't give up easily. She felt that eventually Eddie would give in, and it may very well be soon. His objection to the fertility test was that local eyes and ears might learn about his test and spread the news through town. He could just as easily have the test done in Cincinnati or Columbus, Ohio.

Her daily routine began. She laid out boxers and retired his briefs, placed a vitamin E and a B complex beside his morning meal, and counted the days in her cycle. She made sure they had sex on certain days, insisting on varying positions. In case there was a problem in the transportation of the sperm on their trip to her fallopian tubes, they would have alternate highways.

Nothing worked. The sperm either got lost or didn't do their job when they arrived. After three months, she decided the best bet was Cincinnati. One morning, she made sure Eddie was up bright and early, and there was no morning church meeting.

She prepared blueberry pancakes and real bacon, not turkey substitute. When Eddie walked into the kitchen, she said, "Honey, sit down. I'll get your coffee."

Finding the paper, he waited for his coffee. After she set down the cup, she sat across from him.

"We haven't had a vacation in three years. How would you like to go to Cincinnati? They have a great zoo and two wonderful amusement parks. There's Coney Island with the big roller coaster and King's Island with the water rides. We haven't done anything fun in a long time. I want to go."

He considered that. "It might be a month or so before I can get it into my schedule. Sure, why not?"

Her trap was baited. After a month passed, she said, "Eddie, while we're in Cincinnati, I'd like us both to visit a fertility clinic. They have one of the best in the nation. You do want children, don't you?"

"Why, of course I do."

"Then you'll do it?"

"I'll consider it."

Six weeks later, in central Cincinnati, the two of them walked up to a gray stone building that had been built in the 1930's. Inside, they found the fertility lab, where they separated and saw different doctors.

They had their results the following day. Both of them had issues. His sperm were weak swimmers and didn't move well, and some carried anti-sperm antibodies. At some point in his life, he might have been injured in the epididymis, the organ that manufactured, stored, and delivered the sperm.

"It's not that bad," the balding, obese, middle-aged doctor explained, pointing at a poster-sized male penis with all the supporting parts color coded with fancy Latin names. "They still work, and they still get out. They're just not vigorous or well-populated. In the right situation, they'll work."

Beverly, however, produced plenty of eggs, each ready and receptive for the head of the sperm to attach, but the surface wasn't sticky enough. The eggs were low on a special sugar called SLeX, or Sialyl-lewis-x sequence, that coated the outside of the eggs and was the binding factor. Though Eddie's sperm swimmers were weak, those that reached the eggs bumped into them and bounced off like a fly run over by a billiard ball.

The doctor had a solution for that: in-vitro fertilization. He pulled up another poster-sized chart and explained the concept. Reverend Eddie stopped him in midsentence.

"No child of mine will come from a dish," he declared.

"Oh, no," the doctor said. "The child will come from your wife, and it will be your sperm and her egg. We just join the two in the dish; then, after three to six days in a growth medium, we implant them in her uterus. She will indeed deliver the baby."

"No, thank you," Eddie said firmly and with finality.

The trip back from Cincinnati proved long and silent. His only comment was when he muttered, "We never made it to King's Island."

CHAPTER 10

(Pre-Murder, Edith)

Pastors are revered, giving rise to the term *Reverend*. Sometimes, they are placed on a pedestal and admired as shining examples of the goodness of man. One of the professional quandaries of the vocation is when admiration turns to affection.

Sigmund Freud wrote a paper in 1915 on "transference." He describes a patient who substituted her doctor for her husband. Whether Freud wrote from personal experience or purely academically was never known. If he were personally involved, he never let it slip. The woman he described transferred her feelings for her deceased husband to her psychoanalyst.

In Pleasant Valley, several months before the murder of Rev. Eddie, Edith Black lost her husband to an unusual accident. Ronnie Black, a very fit Huntington fireman, was in a kayak accident on the New River. He and two buddies were running the 6.5-mile section of the lower New River in the spring. Ronnie, in the lead, watched in amazement as the channel ahead became narrowed and blocked by a boulder the size of a locomotive. The swift current sent water off the large rock and cascaded it into white, foamy spray that concluded with a four-foot drop to the Lower Kenney.

Ronnie's kayak slid through the narrow opening and went into free fall toward the pool. Instead of continuing downriver, the kayak was captured by the hydraulic pressure of the waterfall and rotated in place. Ronnie rolled and bobbed up and down in the cold, white water. As hard as he tried, he couldn't break free. Each time he reached the surface, the continuous torrent shoved him back under. Had he understood the mechanics of the situation, he could have stopped fighting and let the hydraulics spit him out the other side. If he were more experienced, he would've waited for the lift portion of the cycle and used a mighty *boof* stroke to propel himself to safety. Unfortunately for him, the water won. His buddies fought their own battles but, somehow, survived to tell the story.

Edith Black chose Pleasant Valley Baptist Church for the funeral. They weren't members, though they attended several times a year. She liked the church's steeple and pristine white paint.

Reverend Eddie treated her with compassion and respect. He was a rock for her, an anchor. Ronnie had been her life, and without him she was lost. She began attending church, then second church, then Sunday school. Within a few weeks, she joined the choir. Whenever the church doors opened, she was there.

Beverly Foxx began noticing Edith after six weeks. One day, after Eddie's cell phone beeped for a text, and Eddie was in the other room, Beverly picked it up.

You coming back to church today?

It was eight o'clock on a Thursday night. There was no service, practice, or any other reason to be at church on such a night.

Beverly didn't say anything as Eddie came into the room. She watched him pick up the phone. He glanced at it, cleared the screen, and turned on the TV. Fifteen minutes later, he was on the back porch making a call.

Over time, he received more calls during the evening hours. By the time he finally understood that Edith was a problem, the situation had already boiled over.

One night, the phone rang during supper. Reverend Eddie answered and said, "Let me step outside, so we can have a better connection."

When he returned to the table, Beverly asked, "Was that Edith Black?"

"Ah...ah, yes. What can I do? She's like a lost puppy looking for a home."

"Precisely. Let's not make it *our* home, Edwin. There is a limit. She has turned you into the man in her life. You need to deal with this right now. Are you sure she doesn't have her eye on you?"

"It never crossed my mind," he said quickly.

"Well, it crossed mine. You need to settle her down. Find her a man. I know it's too soon after Ronnie died; but she has a problem, and we don't need it to become *our* problem."

"Beverly, I assure you it's strictly professional. I'm doing what I need to do as a pastor. She's going through the grieving process. She isn't interested in me. She wants a feeling of belonging."

"Yes, and you belong to me. Don't forget it." She stood, folded her napkin, and walked to the bedroom, shutting the door firmly behind her.

"Honey!" he shouted through the door. "I'm just doing my job. This lady's a bit of a nut case!"

Eddie felt irked that Beverly did not trust him, but it was nice to have an attractive woman interested in him. He took it as a compliment, not a problem, but he worried it might get out of hand. He knew he could handle himself. Many women idolized him—or so he believed.

Putting his thoughts in writing provided him with assurance in his walk with God. Even when doubt crept in, or temptation, or fear.

Dear God,

The Devil's at it again. He placed another appealing woman in my path. I know I'm being tempted, but I can't blame the temptress. She needs my ministering, and at this point in her life, I am her comfort. I am asking for guidance from this entrapment. Take the blinders off my dear wife's eyes, so she can see my trust.

Eddie

CHAPTER 11

(Pre-Murder, New Members)

On the first Sunday morning of July at the close of service, the invitation was given. As a favorite hymn was sung, the invitation was given to join the church by acceptance of the faith or by transferring from another church.

On the last verse of *Just as I Am,* a family of three—mother, father, and teenage daughter—joined the church.

Reverend Eddie stood at the altar to greet them as they came down the aisle. It was always nice to see people promenade to the front during altar call. It meant he did his job well that day. His cool, professional demeanor was interrupted, however, as he reached to accept the woman's hand.

"Emma, is it you?" he spoke softly.

"Yes," she whispered. "It is I."

He squeezed her hand. "Welcome," Rev. Eddie said warmly.

The new members were the O'Connell family. They had recently moved from Beckley, West Virginia, and had bought a four-bedroom home on three-quarters of an acre on Charles Street. Patrick O'Connell, Emma's husband, was an Assistant District Road Supervisor for the West Virginia Department of Highways. Emma, having changed her first name to Wanda, was a registered nurse working at a Huntington Hospital with the Marshall Medical School. April, their daughter, was extremely lovely. Though fifteen, she looked like twenty-one. Like a spring peach, she ripened early.

April assumed her good looks came from her mother since her biological father disappeared when she was two. She saw his photograph once, but the only way she guessed he might be her real father was that he held her and stood beside her mother.

The photo was in an album at her grandmother's home. When she showed the picture to her mother, she smiled and said, "That was a different life."

At fifteen, April felt as if she were on her own second lifetime. She was uprooted at the end of ninth grade when the family moved from Beckley in the southern part of the state to the hick town of Pleasant Valley.

April rarely left her room. She considered hitchhiking back to Beckley but realized it was too dangerous. Even dressed as a boy, she felt some pervert might pick her up and do who-knew-what. She decided to stay in her room and see how few words she could speak with her mother and stepfather over the summer.

By mid June, she was up to twenty-nine words. She kept a record, logging her words each night. She gave herself a special star if the number was zero. After three weeks, she verbalized ten words.

"Do they have a pool in this god-forsaken place?" she asked, wondering if the total was nine words if god-forsaken counted as only one.

Her mother thought it was a good idea for April to get out of the house and meet kids her own age. They took her to Sunday school and church at Pleasant Valley Baptist, but she didn't speak to anyone there, either.

One evening, her mother knocked on April's door. "May I come in?"

The door opened, and April motioned her inside.

"April, this isn't healthy. You can't go the rest of your life without talking."

April looked at her. *Like hell I can't,* she thought.

"I know you think you loved that boy, but the whole group was too old for you. They all had cars and wanted to stay out all night to drink and do all kinds of things. I'm no prude. I've smelled weed before, but it wasn't right."

"Mom...." There was no way she could tell her mother how she felt about Timmy. Her mother wouldn't believe he was different. Why waste the words, when they would only be ignored?

Instead, she patted her mother's hand like her mother had done to her when she was little. Emma's eyes filled with tears.

April kissed her cheek and led her to the door. She was astute in her negotiations, offering a kiss for solitude and a pat on the hand for forgiveness. Tomorrow would start another day, and the cycle would begin again.

The next morning at the breakfast table, April smiled her good morning. Pat, her stepfather, waited until she poured milk over her cereal and raised the spoon to her mouth.

"Hey, Honey. There's a community pool three blocks over and two blocks up toward the high school. I could drop you off."

April shook her head. "Not ready. Thanks."

Pat stood and walked past her, leaning over to kiss the top of her head lightly. "When you are, let me know."

She wasn't ready to leave the house. She wanted freedom to be on her terms. It was a long summer, and she did her best to make it miserable for everyone. She spent hours on her cell phone, talking to her friends in Beckley. She continued the daily silent attack on her parents.

They all settled into a routine. On weekdays, Pat got up at 6:30, had coffee and breakfast, and drove to the Department of Highways office fourteen miles away in Ona at the intersection of Fudges Creek Road and Route 60. Wanda felt as if her life became that of a warden or prison guard.

When Pat returned from work, Wanda and Pat spent the evenings downstairs, while April remained in her room. Pat was the first one to break.

"Wanda," he said one night, "this has to stop. This is no way to live our lives. April must get out of her room, go outside, go to town or the pool. She has to start school in a few more weeks."

Wanda gave him a troubled look. "She isn't going to school."

"What?"

"She refuses. She went online and signed up for home school. Obviously, we have to sign the papers and show we agree. I don't know what else to do. She won't be sixteen until after the school year begins, so we are required to enroll her or have a certified home school solution. I don't know if I have the energy to fight her every morning."

"So, you're just going to give in to her?" he asked angrily.

"No, but I think for the first half of the school year, this might be a good solution. Hopefully, her anger will subside over the next few months. By the first of the year, she'll want to socialize with kids her own age. She can't live in that room forever."

April wasn't Pat's daughter, so it wasn't his call. He decided to find relief outside the home and began attending village council meetings and taking part in local politics. His family life had fallen apart, and it all traced back to Timmy.

CHAPTER 12

(Pre-Murder, Tim and April)

When April was fourteen and they lived in Beckley, she attended a party at her best friend Judy's house where she first met Tim Ferguson, a tall young man who was in college and had his own Mustang convertible, a high-school graduation gift from his grandfather two years before. It was cherry red with black leather interior and black rag top.

Tim was skinny and had a large Adam's apple. At best, he looked like an early version of Clint Eastwood or James Dean, iconic images that were foreign to a ninth grader of the twenty-first century. Still, he was a college man with a car, a dream for a fourteen-year-old.

Tim walked over to April with two drinks in his hand. "So you're April. Judy told me a lot about you. She even showed me your Facebook pictures. They don't do you justice."

"You say I take a bad picture?"

"That's not at all what I said. They were good, but you are better."

April already knew from Judy about her older cousin Timmy who was an engineering student at Marshall. She made him seem a lot more appealing and dynamic than he was in real life.

April was just blossoming, and Tim was at the right place at the right time. The fact that he was five years older didn't enter the equation. He had experienced no social life during his high school years. He was a skinny, studious nerd. Girls didn't notice him, and boys avoided.

In honor of Tim's graduation, his grandfather handed him the keys to the Mustang. It was a thing of beauty, irresistible to look upon even if the owner wasn't. The car became his mojo; though even with that boost, most college girls gave him no more than a smile and a wave.

April had matured beyond her years. And she always liked boys, and they her; but suddenly, she had the assets to go along with her personality, making a dangerous combination.

"Are you going to take me for a ride or not?" she teased.

"Anywhere you like. Hop in."

"I've got to be back in an hour. Let's get a pizza."

As he pulled from the parking lot, he looked at her perfectly shaped, tan legs leading to a show-stopping body and mentally thanked his grandfather many times.

The hour passed quickly. On the way back, he asked her to the movies for the next night.

"Sure," she smiled, "but my parents are strict. It has to be a double date, and you will have to be a junior at Beckley High and only sixteen."

"No problem," Tim agreed quickly.

That wasn't the first lie she told her parents, and it wouldn't be the last.

At what point does a rock become a diamond or a lump of coal? Both are carbon based, and both are created under a lot of pressure, but each has its own destiny. It is the same way with people. They are also carbon-based and under strong pressure, though each person has his own fate. Does nature or nurture turn someone into whoever they are? Is it genes from DNA or blue jeans that turns someone in one direction or another?

April was a loved and loving child. Wanda was her role model; and Pat, her stepfather, was firmly wrapped around her little finger. She was the center of their world and they hers until she reached middle school, when the blue jeans took control. She wore them two sizes too small. April and Wanda had fights almost daily about the proper way to dress for school.

Then the fight moved on to boys. April was smart enough to downplay the issue. She made good grades and participated in school activities. She rarely dated, even to a movie or a dance. Most of her social life consisted of get-togethers, a benign name for parties.

The latest thing was dating boys with cars. The rules were strict: Home by eleven and accompanied by another couple at all times. There would be no beer or alcohol.

April introduced Tim as the sixteen-year-old cousin of her friend, Judy, with whom they were double-dating to see a movie. Although dubious when they met, Pat and Wanda felt he made a good impression and said, "Be careful, and be back at eleven."

They turned April over to Tim for the evening.

Once at the movie theater, Tim let his passengers out. Judy and Jay, her date, would see the movie, and Tim promised to pick them up on time after their show. He and April intended to take a drive in the country but ended up parked in a remote location on a county road.

At first, they just kissed, but the situation quickly escalated, and April soon matriculated into the ways of college without needing to pay for the tuition.

It was a game changer for April. The rest of the summer passed in a whirlwind of activity. Tim and April were together constantly. September would come quickly, and he had to return to Marshall University, while April must finish high school. Typically, such a romance burned out with distance and the passage of time, but this thing with April was real. He knew college meant heavy studies necessary for his professional future. His life would never get better than spending this summer with April.

He came up with the perfect plan to extend their relationship. She had to find out if there was any way she could slip off for a few days to go to Hilton Head, South Carolina. His grandfather had a condo near the beach that was unoccupied for most of the winter months.

When he presented the idea in late August, April laughed.

"Are you kidding?" she asked. "What am I supposed to tell my parents? 'Tim and I want to spend a long weekend together?' I don't think that'll work."

Tim was desperate for any glimmer of hope to prolong the affair. "I just wanted you to know about it. Something may come up. You never know."

He was right. Six weeks later Pat told his family of his impending promotion. He would be given a bonus and a permanent record citation for his innovative work in producing a contingency plan for the Division of Highways during severe and hazardous conditions.

Patrick's original thinking involved coordination with the Federal Government and the National Guard, and his program earned the state substantial federal funding for its implementation. He and other notable state employees would present their papers at a seminar at Greenbrier in White Sulphur Springs, West Virginia, in mid-November.

April told her mother it would be a good retreat for Wanda and Patrick to enjoy together. She'd stay with Judy. April even had Judy's mother call Wanda and say they'd be pleased to have April stay with them for a few days.

It was arranged that the O'Connell's would spend four days at the Luxury Resort in Greenbrier, paid for by the State of West Virginia, while April would be with the Fergusons.

Once her parents left, though, April called Mrs. Ferguson and said there was a change of plans. She wanted to see her stepfather receive his award, so she had decided to go along to White Sulphur Springs with them. But, of course, she did not.

Tim and April had a wonderful three days. The condo had a magnificent ocean view. The salt air stirred the blood and rejuvenated their young passion. For three days, April was wined and dined like a princess. There was nothing Tim's American Express card couldn't buy. They had no worries or problems until a North Carolina state trooper's lights flashed in their rearview mirror just north of Greensboro on the return ride.

"Don't worry, April," Tim said, pulling over. "I didn't do anything wrong."

When the officer approached Tim's window, Tim said nervously, "Sir, I don't think I was speeding."

"That's not why I pulled you over. May I see your driver's licenses? You, too, Miss." He looked across at April.

She knew she was in trouble. "I don't have one."

"How old are you?" he asked in an official voice.

"Sixteen."

He studied her closely. "Then you must be the wrong girl. I'm looking for a fifteen-year-old. Is your name April?"

"Yes…OK…well, uh, yes, I'm fifteen, she stammered. Has something happened? Are my parents alright?"

Looking at her sternly, but addressing Tim, the officer glanced at the driver's license. "According to this," Mr. Ferguson," "you're twenty-one."

"Yes. What's the problem?"

"You ever heard of the Mann Act? You're in violation of it, and I have to take you to the station."

"What? Are you arresting me?"

"Yes, and I'm detaining the young lady, too."

"Can I make a call?" Tim took his cell phone from his pocket.

The trooper shook his head. "Not now. Time for that later. Mr. Timothy Ferguson, you're under arrest for violation of the Mann Act, transporting a woman across a state line for immoral purposes. You are also under arrest for contributing to the delinquency of a minor."

As the officer read him his rights and handcuffed him, April was in tears. She had pushed the envelope, and it exploded in her face.

The officer placed them both in his car, with Tim in the backseat and April in the front. He didn't handcuff or arrest her. The Mann Act came from a 1932 Supreme Court case where it was determined that the woman carried across the state line, with or without her consent, would not be punished for her acquiescence. April's punishment would come at home.

April sat quietly, glancing toward the back seat occasionally at Tim. Where had the perfect plan gone wrong?

CHAPTER 13

(Pre-Murder, Perfect Plan)

As the O'Connell's headed toward home along Route 52, they saw a sign for the Greenbrier County Apple Festival.

"Oh, Pat, let's go to that," Wanda said excitedly. "I'd like to get a bag of apples for Judy's family to thank them for looking after April. Maybe I'll even bake an apple pie."

Patrick pulled the car over. "You should call them first and see if they like apple pies. They may prefer cherry, pumpkin or …"

Wanda affectionately slapped him on the shoulder. "Everyone loves apple pie, but it is a good idea to call and let them know we are on our way home."

Mrs. Ferguson answered the phone. After pleasantries were exchanged, Wanda asked if April was close by for a quick hello.

Mrs. Ferguson, stunned, didn't know what to say; but, as one mother to another, she had to tell the truth. She took a deep breath. "You mean April isn't with you?"

"No. She's there, isn't she?" Wanda began to panic.

"No. She called last week and said her plans changed, because you wanted her to go to the ceremonies. I think it was on Wednesday."

Wanda felt her hand shaking. Where was her daughter? *Oh, April, you stupid child!* "May I speak with Judy?"

Judy answered a moment later.

"Judy, this is important, and a lie won't be tolerated. Do you know where April is?"

"Not really," she fudged.

"Do you know who she's with?"

"Probably Tim, but I don't know. She told me she was leaving for a few days. I didn't know what she meant, but I decided not to ask."

"Please put your mother back on the phone," Wanda said coldly.

Over the next few minutes, Wanda got the number of Tim's parents. And within fifteen minutes, she had contacted the police. Five hours later, Tim was in custody, and Pat and Wanda were on their way to Greensboro, North Carolina.

That incident and the subsequent restraining order against Tim Ferguson were the tipping point for the family to leave the Beckley area. Pat hated moving. He was in line to become regional superintendent, but Wanda was determined and insisted they not only move but make sure they had a restraining order against Tim.

James Madison Ferguson, the patriarch of the family, owned a large stake in coal mines and mineral rights throughout West Virginia. When he heard that Tim, his only grandson, was arrested for taking a woman across a state line for immoral reasons, he wanted to laugh. It was about time that boy started acting like a man. He hired a top lawyer and got the charges dismissed. Tim Ferguson returned to Marshall without even a slap on the wrist.

Wanda knew the problem extended beyond Tim Ferguson. It was the entire setting—friends, parties, drugs, and things Wanda didn't want to think about. April had to be reborn, and she knew the man to do it.

Moving to Pleasant Valley and joining the Baptist Church was no accident. It was a calculated choice.

CHAPTER 14

(Pre-Murder, Apologies)

The Monday morning after the O'Connell's joined the church, Reverend Eddie found the contact card for the family and called their home number.

"Wanda, this is Eddie. It was so great to see you after all these years."

"You, too," she replied.

"I was surprised and overwhelmed. You know we change as we grow older. I want to apologize for how our relationship ended. I was a jerk. I didn't intend to be; but looking back, it was, of course, as much my doing as yours. I was so dumb about how the world worked back then. Again, I apologize."

"Apology accepted," Wanda responded. "It hurt for a long time after you walked away. I quit school, because I didn't want to see you on campus. Yes, jerk is one of the names I called you, but a lot has happened since; and as you say, we grow. My life saw many changes as well. I think you're a good man, and I'll seek your help when needed."

Eddie thought for a moment before answering. This wasn't a typical situation with a new church member. He had history with Wanda.

He reverted to his pastoral preferences. "I look forward to helping any way I can. Please feel free to come to the church any time. Was your husband, Pat, transferred here?"

"Sort of. He's with the State Road, and there was an opening in the Barboursville and Ona offices. We needed a change of environment for our daughter, so he took the position."

Eddie felt more comfortable and back in control. "We're glad to have you. As I said, my door is always open."

As he hung up, he mused over what might have been and felt strangely uneasy.

CHAPTER 15

(Pre-Murder, April)

April felt the move was an act of war. She was determined to be as uncooperative as possible. She resisted any acceptance of the new home, area, or lifestyle. In her passive-aggressive position, she boxed herself into a twelve-by-fourteen room, her only contact with the outer world through her cell phone. Every day, she called Judy in Beckley to catch up on news and to wallow in how bad her life was as a prisoner.

One day, a couple weeks into her self-imposed solitary confinement, April received a call from Judy.

"April, you'll never win your freedom by staying housebound."

"What do you mean? I'm making their lives miserable."

"Look at the cost. You have no life."

"True. What would you do?"

"Well, you've gone too far to just give up. But think about it. So what if you agreed to go to Pleasant Valley High. A normal high school life rather than online schooling. Sounds like more fun to me."

"Yes, but my mother's idea of a normal high school life is quite different from mine."

"Well, let her think you're accepting it on her terms. The less said, the better. You have a lot of wiggle room if you don't pin her down to rules and terms."

April considered that. "These walls *are* closing in on me. Overall, that's not a bad idea. I will wait for the right time to spring the trap. My mother's different here than back home. We joined the Baptist Church, and we've always been Methodist."

"She might be trying to keep you off balance."

"I don't know, but she's up to something. She forces me to go to church. She even threatened to stop cooking for me if I didn't go. Weird."

"Any boys at church?"

"Hardly."

What April did not know was her mother's recent visit to the Reverend Edwin Foxx.

CHAPTER 16

(Pre-Murder, Wanda and Rev. Eddie)

About ten days after joining the church, Wanda appeared at the pastor's office door. His secretary had apparently gone to the restroom or to the kitchen for coffee. She knocked on the open door and stuck her head in to look around. Pastor Foxx was on his knees behind his desk, not praying but looking for a book at the bottom of his 10-shelf library that took up a full wall in his office. Her feet and ankles first came into his vision and then her leg. It caught his attention, and he peered around the desk to see Wanda standing in his doorway.

"May I come in? I know I should have called but...."

He cut her off in mid-sentence. "No appointment necessary. Come right in and have a seat. I was just looking for a quote, probably easier to find it on the computer, but I like the old-fashioned way. So, what can I do for you?"

She smiled and sat as he pulled himself up and found his seat on the other side of the desk.

"Do you mind if I shut the door?" she asked.

"No problem. I'll tell Sandra that I'll be a few minutes." He stepped out and then came right back and shut the door behind him, motioning Wanda over to the couch.

"I don't want to feel like a teacher or a counselor. This will be a lot better."

She sat facing him on the sofa.

"This is odd. Do I call you Reverend Foxx or Reverend Eddie, or what?"

"Whatever makes you feel more at ease. Reverend Eddie seems to please most."

Wanda squirmed in her seat, sighed, and began. "Reverend Eddie, prior to coming to Pleasant Valley we were Methodists for a long time, but had no need personal enough to require the Pastor's assistance. And I know in the Catholic Church that anything said between the Priest and the parishioner is held sacred and secret. Is that the way it is with Baptists?"

"If you're asking if I can talk to you in confidence and keep it between us, the answer is yes."

"Well, Reverend Eddie, no one knows what I'm about to say but me. My husband doesn't know it; my daughter doesn't know it. So, I am trusting you. The truth is that April is your daughter." She blurted it out without even a pause.

Edwin Foxx stopped breathing, his eyes widened, and a slow tremble spread through his extremities, but oh, how strived to appear and seem calm and unaffected. It took him a moment to speak. "Are you sure?"

"One hundred percent," Wanda said as she looked deep into his eyes.

He returned the look, but his insides were fluttering. He knew he had to be careful in questing Wanda about her motives for not telling him all these years. He had a hundred questions, but probably this was not the right time to ask them.

"So, your moving to Pleasant Valley was no accident?"

Wanda was over the hard part, and her answers came easy, because she knew what she had to do.

"I wanted the transfer, because April had gotten into the wrong group of kids. They were older and into sex and drugs and everything. When my husband got enough seniority, I knew we could move to the Cabell County Division. I knew where you were the church pastor, and I know you're a good man."

"So, what do you want of me?" Edwin asked.

"I want you to be her pastor. Totally in the Biblical sense, I want you to be the shepherd that gives her guidance that keeps her safe."

"Of course, I'll do that." Before he could say anything else, Wanda broke in.

"This has to be our secret. Pat does not know. And as I said, April does not know, nor should she. They both believe she's the daughter of my first husband Mike. I met him shortly after I left Alderson Broaddus. He was nice and I was pregnant. He didn't know, and I needed a husband. Well, I don't need to spell out the rest to you. The marriage lasted a year. My parents could tolerate an ill-advised marriage but not an illegitimate granddaughter. So, now you do what you have to do to reach April for a better way."

Eddie reached across the couch and took her hand. "You can count on me. I'm sorry it all happened this way, but now we have the future. I'll be there, and no one will ever know. Let's pray." He lowered himself to his knees with his elbows resting on the couch.

"Our dear beloved Father, we thank you for everything. We thank you for April and for Wanda and her courage. Give me the strength and the wisdom to guide and mentor my child in Your ways. We as sinners have fallen and come short. Allow Wanda and me to carry this secret, not in shame but in love. A love for You and for our child. It is in Jesus' name I ask. Amen."

He stood, reached over, and squeezed Wanda's hand.

"Thank you for bringing her to me."

Wanda let herself out with tears streaming down her cheeks.

The Reverend went back to the seat at his desk. As he sat down, the first thought that crossed his mind was the futility of the Cincinnati trip to the fertility clinic. *I knew I wasn't shooting blanks. My briefs are going back in the drawer.*

CHAPTER 17

(Pre-Murder, April and Church)

In a way, attending church was like being placed in a penalty box for April. In another way, it was an escape. The church was neutral ground for April and her mother. The Pleasant Valley Baptist Church had an iconic steeple of pristine white above a large brick-and-wood building. The church sanctuary originally held four hundred people. But under Reverend Eddie's ministry, the congregation grew much larger. The house was always packed even with the additional morning services.

Most Baptists tried to make it to Sunday services. Dedicated members went four times on Sunday and once on Wednesday night. Sunday School classes met first. The two worship services followed. Then at 6:00 p.m., the Deacons' wives hosted a fellowship and refreshment time for adults while the youth groups met separately. The last Sunday worship service began at 7:30 p.m. The O'Connell's went to all of them. It made for a full Sunday.

April looked forward to the Sunday evening Baptist Youth Fellowship. Shortly after her first visit, she was asked to be one of the leaders. It was a new role for her. In Beckley, she ran with an older crowd and was a follower. Here, she was a leader, mostly because of Reverend Eddie. For some reason, he took a special interest in her, seeking her out and welcoming her participation. He complimented her on her ideas, encouraging her to take a bigger role in the program.

April was careful to seem aloof when in front of her mother. Sometimes during a sermon, though, she paid attention and followed what the preacher said. John 3:16 tugged at her heart.

There was a safety net around her at church, almost like being in fantasy land or an unreal world. The other kids weren't intimidating, and her mother transformed into a more moderate temperament. Always, the sermon discussed the fight between good and bad, God and the devil. In the long run, God always prevails, Rev. Eddie says. But the devil puts up a good fight.

From April's viewpoint, it was OK to step over the line. As she turned sixteen, God seemed bland, and life needed some spice. Anyway, God would ultimately win, and April would transition into her mother. She prayed God would at least give her ten years before that happened. *"For God so loved the world ..."* Why did that verse flash through her mind?

CHAPTER 18

(Pre-Murder, Exceptional Wife)

A preacher's wife's life is like playing Ed McMahon to Johnny Carson or Gabby Hayes to Roy Rogers. If those comparisons sound old and chauvinistic, that simply reflects Southern Baptist society. It was a good ol' boys' club as far as ministers went. A woman's place wasn't behind the pulpit but behind the man behind the pulpit. Scripture forbade women pastors.

Paul once said, *"But suffer not a woman to teach, nor to usurp authority over the man, but to remain silent."* [Timothy 2:12]

In Corinthians 14:33-35, Paul again set forth the requirements for an orderly church.

> *For God is not a God of confusion but of peace,*
> *as in all the churches of the saints. The women*
> *are to keep silent in the churches; for they are not*

permitted to speak, but are to subject themselves, just as the Law also says.

If they desire to learn anything, let them ask their own husbands at home; for it is improper for a woman to speak in church.

It always secretly troubled Beverly that Southern Baptists never considered the Biblical times and laws of the land when women, even now, were directed never to speak in church. After all, when Jesus walked the earth, women were property belonging in ownership by men. Even though Jesus' teachings equaled women to men and even though He showed Himself to women first after He arose from the grave, the New Testament writers seemed to ignore what Christ Himself attempted to honor. Customs were too ingrained she supposed. Oh, Southern Baptists came across respectful enough. After all, Sunday School needs teachers. The choir needs singers. Money must be raised for missions and building projects. And hot meals and supper desserts make fellowship memories. However, other denominations have recognized long ago the power of Christ through women speakers, and some even stand behind the pulpit. But not Baptists.

Oh, well, one shouldn't be too hard on Southern Baptists. "Simply following doctrine," they say. And there is indeed a place for women in the church; and that place is behind the men, or at least on the right-hand side of the pew.

The unwritten rules of ministers' wives set them apart. They shouldn't be too attractive, but look nice, like maybe a seven on a scale of ten. A minister's wife should be appallingly skinny or fifteen or more pounds overweight. Blondes and redheads need not apply unless they were willing to tone down their hair color a bit. Also, a preacher's wife should be at least two inches shorter than her husband.

There were always exceptions, but anyone who attends a Southern Baptist convention could look around and see the criteria.

Beverly wasn't the exception, though she was exceptional. She was an encyclopedia of knowledge who knew a compendium of current events as well as events from the past five years. She remembered who said what to whom regardless of the occasion.

Most of all, she remembered sermons. Her job in the church was to sit in the second row to the left of the preacher. When he turned his head left to right while speaking, she could establish eye contact. He avoided it and tried to look past her; but often, their eyes met, and she either smiled in approval or frowned in disapproval. With two Sunday sermons, she had a double opportunity to critique. It was a self-appointed job, without compensation, but brought plenty of satisfaction.

At the dinner table one Sunday evening, Beverly asked in a knowing voice, "Edwin, wasn't the message this morning a redo of one from last year?"

"I don't think so. It was different text and a different direction." He turned the page of the newspaper he read.

"No, I think it was the same text. I know it was the same inappropriate joke."

"You mean the one about what to call a one-legged woman in West Virginia?" He smiled.

"Precisely. How could you do that? We have a woman in the church with that affliction."

"Yeah. Ilene Taylor. She's the one who told me that joke."

he laughed.

"That doesn't excuse it."

He knew it was his wife's way of participating and was accustomed to constructive criticism. It kept him on his toes, but that day, he had a slip of the tongue, which opened a new dynamic in his marriage.

In a mildly sarcastic tone, he retorted, "Maybe you should provide me with appropriate jokes or anecdotes to lead into my sermons."

"What a wonderful idea!"

He hoped she was kidding, but he knew better. He accidentally opened the door to his private sanctum.

"Do you have a story or a joke tonight?" she asked immediately.

"No. Tonight should be jokeless, just your standard John 3:16. Not much you can do with that. The text says it all." He prayed that would end the conversation.

The following Monday morning at breakfast, Beverly asked about the theme for the coming Sunday sermon.

"I'll stick with John 3:16. You can't go wrong with it. I'm not sure, though. I'm in the middle of a series about making our workplaces God's workplace."

"Well, consider this. Why did the spider cross the road?"

"I don't know," he said, exasperated.

"To get to his website."

Eddie smiled, knowing if he included the joke in his sermon, his wife would be pleased, but at what cost? How could he include *website* with the words: *For God so loved the world that He gave His only begotten Son?*

CHAPTER 19

(Pre-Murder, Custodian)

A city, town, or village is a population of people who have differences and similarities. Jim Spurlock, the church custodian, stood five-feet-ten and was stocky, his hands callused from hard, honest work. He wasn't remarkable in any way except for his nose, which was the appropriate size but, unfortunately, not in the proper place. One kind description for it could be equine. Another might be the phrase, "God missed when he put that one on." Otherwise, Jim was a handsome gent of forty. His athletic build waned in the past few years due to lack of exercise; but to Jim, when he looked in the mirror, all was good. Unfortunately, it wasn't.

His marriage hit a rough spot, and the beautiful girl he met at a family reunion was slowly sliding out of his life. Theirs had been a wonderful romance when they found out they weren't remotely related. Friendship turned to interest and, finally, love. Then as years went by, it all reversed. At first, it was with acceptance and patience, then tolerance, then resentment. Finally, the only feeling left became charity.

Jim and Sandra, his wife of eighteen years, had been living separately for the past year; and it became a comfortable situation. Neither secretly were seeing other people, and they even still had occasional sex. The situation was actually better than the final year they had lived together. She talked of his moving back in; but when he agreed, she found reasons to delay it until the following month or possibly later in the summer.

She loved him, but there were times when she didn't like him. He wasn't easy to live with. It was more than a toilet seat being up or down. He left his shoes on the bed, dirty underwear on the floor, and he had the attitude that as a woman, she had to listen to him no matter what.

She lived that way before, when her father was the dominant male, and her mother accepted it like a saint. Sandra didn't want her parents' marriage. She wanted a man who cared for her because she was the most important thing in his world. Even more, she didn't want to be taken care of. She wanted respect, trust, love, and ample money. With Jim, there was little money, a trifle of respect, a smidgeon of trust, and love only on birthdays, Christmas, and Friday nights. It wasn't enough.

She wondered if it was greedy to want more. She wanted a fulfilled life, running over with happiness, contentment, self-satisfaction, and the inner peace of knowing she was alive, not just living.

She married Jim eighteen years earlier when she was twenty-two. They were full of love and expectations, but the love mellowed, and the expectations were like penny balloons with tiny holes that always fizzled out. Life fell into a routine of marching from one day to the next, one month to the next, and one season to the next. Suddenly, she realized she was forty, and she was childless, loveless, and hopeless.

On the morning of her fortieth birthday, she stood in front of the bathroom mirror stark naked. Though she was critical in her assessment, she was pleased overall. She looked good at five-feet-six-inches tall and still had an attractive figure.

Drinking coffee alone at the kitchen table, her assessment of her lifestyle was one of failure and missed opportunities. Her body held up well, but her life was sagging.

Sandra and Jim worked at Pleasant Valley Baptist Church for the past five years. Both were only part-time. She was the church secretary, while Jim was the handyman and janitor. In a way, her job was superior to his. She wrote the paycheck and outlined what jobs needed doing.

Oddly, it was the church that led to their separation. Jim had difficulty accepting orders from his wife, even though they originated with the pastor or the deacon board. He didn't like the attention visitors paid to Sandra. Most of all, the pastor treated Jim like hired help while treating Sandra as a friend and equal.

They hid their separation from the church, because Baptists didn't believe in divorce. Besides, Jim felt it was temporary. Sandra hadn't found anything new she wanted to do.

Their marital problems began over an innocent incident. Sandra was friendly to the new volunteer choir director, a man of thirty-four. From Jim's viewpoint, friendliness ended and flirtation began. In his opinion, she dressed too nice for church work. Her hair was perfect, her skirt was above the knee, and her blouse a little too tight. She looked like a woman preparing for a date.

The more he observed, the more he obsessed. Did she smile the same for women as for men? Was her smile bigger for younger men than older men? In his mind, the answers were yes.

One day, as they prepared to go to church in their separate vehicles, he stopped her car in the driveway.

"Sandra, you aren't wearing that to church." He pointed at her dress.

"Yes, I am."

"Are you doing this to spite me?"

"No. I'm doing it because it's clean." She smirked.

"That's our dress, the one you always wear on our anniversary."

She groaned, shook her head, and went inside to change.

That night, she said she still loved him, but the spark was gone. He only noticed her if another man looked at her. What happened to her friend, the happy, trusting husband? When had the joy flown away?

"We aren't kids anymore," he replied. "We both turned forty last year. Life's good. We have each other. I hope you know I love you, but I have to be me. I can't be Prince Charming all the time. This isn't a fairytale. It takes both of us working to keep things going. I need some down time. I'm sorry you can't accept that."

It wasn't what she wanted to hear, but it was what she expected. She loved him, too, but he was like a pair of old, comfortable shoes.

One week later, they had a silly argument over a broken coffee cup. Sandra broke it, and it was one of Jim's favorites, one he had before they even met. Sweeping up the pieces, she asked him to leave.

"Just give me space," she said. "I don't want to live like this. Just a few weeks to clear the air."

Weeks became months, and the air was still stale.

CHAPTER 20

(Pre-Murder, Mug & Plate)

Small towns like Pleasant Valley have few choices for day-to-day shopping, restaurant, and grocery stores. They don't have Starbucks on every corner. Pleasant Valley didn't even have one. If Starbucks moved in, it would have trouble competing with the Mug and Plate, where coffee was served in a white porcelain mug with a slightly narrow waist. They were the color of fresh cream and made coffee seem robust and tasty, as well as keeping liquids hot longer. There was no logo on the side, but the plates matched the creamy white color. No saucers were used, either. The restaurant was mug land. Food was good, servings were full, and prices reasonable.

Nancy White, a sixty-eight year old native West Virginian, was the founder, proprietor, hostess, and cashier at the Mug. On many days, she worked as cook and waitress. She was born in Dingess, West Virginia, in a two-story wood house with tin roof and a long front porch that emptied to one side with six steps toward a flat piece of ground.

Her childhood home, like many in West Virginia, rested in a notch cut from the side of a mountain. For most of the day, it saw no sun. A blacktop road, fifty feet from the elevated front porch, wiggled past the front of the house; it found its way to the abandoned Dingess railroad tunnel that was half a mile long and one lane wide.

The tunnel was the high point of life in Dingess and its only claim to fame. After growing up in rural Mingo County, Nancy, even at sixty-eight, felt blessed to work twelve hours a day in a business she owned. She and her ex-husband started it from scratch and ran it together until he ran off with one of the waitresses when the village was just beginning to bloom. When she heard of his death, she merely said, "Bless his soul," with an undeniable sadness. She worked long hours with small profits, but the rewards were large. The Mug and Plate was the heart of Pleasant Valley.

CHAPTER 21

(Pre-Murder, Ray-Bob)

A village isn't a village without an idiot. The unspoken election for that award in Pleasant Valley went to Raymond Robert Raymond in a landslide. He wasn't stupid—far from it. He was smart, very bright, and highly opinionated. He had a bumper sticker on his Ford 150 truck that read:

I Love My Country!
It's the Government I Hate.

He wasn't a member of the Tea Party, because they were too tame. "They're political," he often said. "How can you be political and be against the government?"

Ray-Bob, as most called him, was the village barber. It was a good thing he was a good barber, but it was even better that he was the only barber in twenty miles. People tolerated his right-of-right-wing lectures as part of the haircut experience. As one village elder said, "It's the only place you can go and get your ears lowered (along with possibly your IQ) for a mere five dollars."

Ray-Bob was a true believer. He was sincere in his beliefs, though he was often sincerely wrong. The one thing he knew for sure was the back and front of a man's head. In twenty years, he had cut thousands of heads of hair. Every single one was different, following the saying, "A man never steps into the same river twice." He felt he never cut the same head of hair twice.

He knew most of his clients by name and could recall the lay of each person's hair, any rooster tails, or cowlicks. His memory was as sharp as his razor. When a man sat in Ray-Bob's chair, an unfinished conversation, argument, or lecture resumed as easily as turning around and picking up the scissors from the alcohol dip. It might have been three or six weeks since he last saw the person, but Ray-Bob was always able to continue the conversation.

Most men left with a laugh and a shake of the head, saying, "That Ray-Bob is one of a kind—I hope."

What they didn't consider was that he was a complex man. There were many layers to his personality, but all were below the surface. His bluster, hate of government, and antisocial feelings were just the lid over a deeper container.

Sundays and Wednesdays were his two off days, when he had no hair to cut and no one to listen to him vent. Those were his days of solitude in the cabin he inherited on the Mud River just outside Milton, West Virginia, twelve miles from Pleasant Valley. The cabin was made of pine logs and rough-cut timber chinked with clay, dried grass, pebbles, sand, and lime from the banks of the Mud. The cabin dated to the nineteen-teens, just after World War One. His great grandfather on his father's side built it on government-granted land. The water came from a well, and the sewer was a septic system. Electricity gave the only touch of civilization, added in 1949.

It wasn't very large, but the cabin provided solitude. The only sound of man was an occasional distant train whistle, as a C&O engine pulled its hundred cars of coal through the valleys, hills and forests on its way through Teays Valley on to the Kanawha Valley.

In the years Ray-Bob owned that cabin, no visitor ever set foot in it. It was his private space. His life was alone except for touching the heads of men. He sought little interaction with people. He didn't cut women's hair, so he rarely spoke to a woman except to say, "Over easy and the coffee is black. Save the sugar, and don't bring a bunch of those cream things."

He wasn't anti-woman, just non-woman. He wasn't gay or straight. He just was. His life suited him, and that was for whom he lived.

One of Ray-Bob's favorite customers was Reverend Eddie. They agreed on nothing.

"Do this unto the least of them, and you have done it unto me," Ray-Bob told Eddie. "What does that mean?" he asked, baiting the preacher. "Honestly, Reverend, do we want a nation of takers?"

"No, but we need givers in our country," Reverend Eddie replied. "We weren't all created equal. Each has his or her talents, but some have limitations and need help. Others have the capacity to help. Charity is a good thing for the receiver and the giver."

"Sounds like a better deal for the receiver." He clipped some hair.

"No, I disagree. It feels good to give."

"Remember that when you leave your tip."

They saw each other each month for several years before Reverend Eddie asked, "Hey, Ray-Bob, how come I never see you in church?"

"Don't go. Don't believe in it."

"You don't believe in God?"

"Didn't say that. I don't believe in man tellin' me what God should be tellin' me."

The pastor heard that line before. "I don't channel God. I don't represent that I speak for Him. I ask the church to listen for God. My job is to give guidance here on earth, to assist when called upon, and to stay out the way when not." He smiled.

"Well, Preacher, I like that last part about staying out of the way. You, now, I believe I could probably tolerate an hour of churchgoing every week. It's the other pew-fillers, shouting "Amen" or standing with a semi-Nazi salute on Sunday and then leaving the building to misbehave themselves in one way or another the rest of the week. You know—the Sunday Christians. Not me, not ever."

"Give us a try. It might surprise you."

"Thanks, but no thanks. Sunday's my day to be with God my way. I know He's up on Mud River. I'm not so sure He's down here."

"You don't think God is at my Baptist Church?"

"Maybe, maybe not. Don't get me wrong. You seem to be a good man, but some of the people in your congregation, well, I don't think they'd know God if He walked through that door."

Ray-Bob shaved Reverend Eddie's neck hair with a straight razor.

"You could be right," Reverend Eddie said. "Just because you don't go to church doesn't mean you're not saved. Just because you don't attend doesn't mean you're on your way to hell; but, in general, I believe church people have a better chance of walking closer with Him."

Ray-Bob tipped Reverend Eddie's head back to shave his neck hairs and finished the shave. When a man had a razor to another man's throat, it was probably best not to argue with him too strongly. "Reverend, I'm in heaven every Wednesday and Sunday. When I'm at the cabin on Mud River, I enjoy squirrel hunting with my bow, fishing, boating, listening to nature and reviving my mind. Solitude and nature are my regeneration. No preaching for me. No disrespect intended."

"None taken." He realized he wouldn't win. Ray-Bob believed in simple truths, and the prospects of changing his mind were minimal. It was better to use his ministerial talents on people who would listen or at least pretend to do so.

Although the conversation ended, an event occurred that changed both men's lives, as well as those of the people around them, in a profound way: The reverend left his reading glasses at the barber shop.

When Reverend Eddie couldn't find his glasses later in the morning to prepare his sermon outline for Sunday, he realized he left them at the barber shop.

"Sandra, are you going to lunch at the Mug?" he asked his secretary.

"Probably. I hadn't thought about it. You need something?"

"I think I left my reading glasses at the barber shop. I tried calling Ray-Bob, but he rarely answers his phone. Would you stop by on your way to lunch and see if they're there?"

"Sure, no trouble at all," she kindly answered.

Ray-Bob was in back, inventorying his hair products, when he heard the door buzzer sounded, as someone opened the front door.

"Be there in a moment!" he called from behind the green, pleated drape separating his storage area from the shop.

When he stepped out, he saw a tall, trim, attractive woman. If she needed a haircut, he would consider changing his policy about women.

"How may I help you?" He parted the curtains for a closer look.

"Reverend Eddie thinks he left his glasses here this morning. He tried to call, but no one answered the phone. He asked if I might stop by on my lunch hour to ask if you have seen any extra glasses lying around?"

Ray-Bob already put them in a drawer, assuming the minister was the owner. Calling or answering phone calls wasn't something he did while a patron was in the chair. He was cutting someone else's hair when he had noticed them, so he tucked the glasses in a safe place.

"I haven't seen any, but I'll look around. Want me to call you if I find them?"

"Yes, please. I could stop by after my lunch." She gave him her number.

As she left, Ray-Bob wondered why he lied about it. He could have reached into the drawer and given them to her, and the fact that he didn't confused him.

Since there was no one else in the shop, he sat in a chair and rotated it until he saw his reflection in the mirror. He used a pair of scissors to trim his nose hair, then he cut back his eyebrows. The situation confused him, but he was quietly moved. He'd seen her before. Pleasant Valley was a small town.

He thought her name was Sandra, but he wondered why he felt as if all the air left the room when he saw her.

Fifteen minutes later, he called her and said, "I found them."

"Great. I'll get them on my way back to the church."

"Excuse me, but you're Sandra, right?"

"Yes."

"Well, Sandra, would you do me a big favor and get me a large sweet tea from the Mug? I'd really appreciate it."

"Sure."

He hung up hoping his twelve-thirty appointment was late.

Sandra brought the iced tea and collected the glasses. The 12:30 appointment was on time, so Ray-Bob had only a moment to make the exchange and give her two dollars for the tea.

"No," she said with a smile. "It's on me."

"Then I owe you lunch."

"Oh, no. thanks, anyway." She walked out.

One week later, Ray-Bob called Sandra at ten-thirty on a Tuesday morning.

"Sandra, this is Ray, the barber. Remember …?"

"Sure. What can I do for you?"

"You can let me buy you lunch today."

"No can do. It wouldn't be proper. I'm married."

"I know that. I cut Jim's hair. Remember, this is a small town."

"Maybe if it were a different town and a different time, I'd say yes."

"OK. Tomorrow at the Rebels and Redcoats in Huntington at twelve-thirty."

"Ray, that's not what I meant."

"Sandra, I say what I mean, and I believe you do, too. Someday and sometime is tomorrow. OK?"

"OK. Someday and sometime, but not tomorrow. Thanks for asking."

She hung up and realized she needed to finalize her situation with Jim. Half a husband was twice as much a problem as a whole one. She hated to hurt him. She still had feelings for him, but they were feelings of kind affection, not love. There was no desire, no passion. The flame flickered and went out. She knew Jim still hoped they could rekindle it. "They had had many good years together, happy ones. Too much for him to walk away from," he expressed many times.

Sandra was the same woman as when she had married Jim. Or was she? What made her change? What created her need for attention now? Surely, the need had always been there, but barely satisfied. As the years went by, her life with Jim turned from any passion to only pacification.

There were no children, but they only fulfilled each other on a minimal level, letting life get between them until there was distance and darkness, and life's travails smothered away the love. They didn't know what happened, and they didn't recognize their participation, but both ended up feeling hollow.

Sandra felt vacant inside, but when a man smiled at her or paid attention to her, she felt a spark, a hint of smoldering, a longing to be cherished.

Jim believed the problem was another man—the preacher. He saw how Reverend Eddie was always in Sandra's office or vice versa. When she was out sick for two days, the church sent her flowers. Jim was out for a week one year earlier with a strained back, received while working at the church, and he hadn't even received a card.

The question was, what could he do to change the situation? At work, he was the custodian, a fancy name for the janitor or the flunky. Should he talk with Reverend Eddie? How could a man of the cloth act in such an underhanded way? If it was just a flirtation, it was still out of line. If it evolved into something more, Jim would handle that, too.

CHAPTER 22

(Pre-Murder, Sandra)

The Reverend was deep into his computer, cross-checking Bible verses to pull together the fragmented ideas he had for that week's sermon when tapping on his door brought him out of his trance.

It was Sandra. "Sir, if you have a moment, I need to talk to you. It's personal."

He turned and gave her his full attention. "Sure. Have a seat. That's what I'm here for."

She rehearsed the words at least ten times in her mind that morning, but sitting there, she didn't know where or how to start.

"You recall a few weeks ago when you asked about Jim and my separation? I'm afraid it's not working out. I love him, but in a very platonic way. I've tried, but every day, it's the same nothingness I feel inside. I wish him well, but I wish he were out of my life.

"After several years of marriage, we accepted that we never had children, and we loved each other. We were a family of two, but it's not that way now. We're friends, and that's the extent of it to me. Isn't it wrong to live a lie?"

Reverend Eddie weighed his words carefully. Sandra didn't know how close to home her situation had hit him. He felt hypocritical that he couldn't tell her how he knew and lived the same feelings with Beverly. He had to assume his role and read his lines like an actor. He would give her the talk and the advice to follow God's plan. He just wished he knew which plan it was.

"Sandra, I'm very sorry to hear this. I commend you for bringing it into the open. No, God doesn't want us to live a lie. Every person's walk with God is different, so there's no universal answer. I wish I could tell you to do this or do that, but it's not that simple. What makes it so difficult is that I have feelings for both you and Jim. More than that, you both are employed here, and I'm sure that's a strain on your marriage. It would be a worse situation if you split completely. Have you told him it's over?"

"Yes and no. Not formally. We've been living separately for a little over a year. A few weeks ago, he asked to move back in, and I said I wasn't ready. He asked if I ever would be ready. I told him I didn't know.

"I know now. I want freedom for both of us. Jim doesn't deserve to be treated like this, but I am hurting him daily. It's easier to go on day-to-day than to face the truth, but now that time has come.

"I know it'll be difficult for you to take sides, which is why I'm telling you this before I talk to him. Here's my letter of resignation. I don't want to put you in a bad situation with him or with the church."

"Whoa! Please reconsider. You're very valued in many ways. We need to think this through and pray about it. I know it's difficult. It took a lot of courage for you to talk to me about it. I can see your words came from your heart. Give me some time, at least overnight. There has to be a better solution."

That evening, Reverend Eddie called Jim on his cell phone. "Can you drop by the office for a minute before you go home?"

The meeting was brief. Reverend Eddie explained that the budget had been revised, and money was tight. The church would be hiring an outside vendor for a weekly cleaning and small jobs as needed. He gave Jim two-weeks' notice. The new cleaning arrangement would start immediately.

Alone, later that night, Rev. Eddie needed to write it down:

Dear God,

It's been awhile. Today, I did something that gives me pause. I terminated the custodian because of his wife. He had no idea of the reason as I most surely do. As I politely spoke the required words, I felt like David dispatching his general to the front lines to be killed, so he could be with Bathsheba. David did it for lust, and I did it for love. The custodian will be OK and should find another job soon.

When I say love, I mean it in the best way--not Eros (sexual)--but affection and friendship. It's hard to separate feelings, emotions, or stirrings. They intertwine like the twisted cone of soft-serve ice cream, where the vanilla and chocolate merge until it's difficult to separate them, but it's all good.

Eddie

CHAPTER 23

(Pre-Murder, Confrontation)

The cold prepared the way for snow; and if it came, it would stick. The concrete sidewalks sparkled with forming ice crystals where the cold fog kissed the surface. Reverend Eddie waited for Ray-Bob, as he arrived to open his shop.

"Hey, Rev. A little early for a haircut. Didn't you get one a week or so ago?"

"I'm not here for a haircut. I need to talk to you."

"Come on in. It's freezing out. I'm sure you don't want to talk on the street."

Entering the shop, they walked into the waiting area. Ray-Bob pointed to a seat, and Reverend Eddie took it.

"Ray-Bob, this thing with Sandra is getting out of hand," he began. "People are beginning to talk. It's not good for her position at the church."

Ray-Bob, seeing the preacher was serious, didn't argue. "I understand. This is a small town with small-minded people, but what she and I do or have is our business. Why should we change, because other people don't like it?"

"Obviously, you don't comprehend the seriousness of adultery."

"I am not an adulterer! I'm not married."

"That's no different. It's a sin. We can't have the church secretary going around town sinning."

"Why not? Everyone else does. I'm in business, because hair grows. You're in business, because people sin." He grinned.

"My job is to stop sin, not condone it. When the Bible says you're forgiven of your sins, that doesn't give you a blank check to commit more. Forgiveness isn't encouragement. The two of you must stop."

"Stop what? Say it. What must we stop?"

"Fornicating," he said in a loud, pulpit voice.

"How do you know we do that? You been peeking?"

"It doesn't matter if you do or don't. It's the appearance of impropriety that places her job in jeopardy. Can't you wait until she's divorced?"

"No, I can't. Furthermore, neither can she. What we do is our business. Working for you doesn't give you ownership. Are you here as her boss or her pastor, or is there something else?"

"I don't like that implication. Mark my word. If you don't stop seeing her, there'll be ramifications."

"Is that a threat?"

"Take it any way you want. Just back off."

"You, Reverend Eddie, are the one who needs to back off. I think you have a thing for Sandra, an unresolved longing. You see her every day. She's close, but you can't have her. You smell her, touch her arm, watch her move, and you know she's off limits. It must be frustrating.

"Then your barber starts seeing her. I understand why you're on your high horse. Maybe the Catholics are right about celibacy. Remember, you're the one married, Rev. Eddie. It would definitely be adultery for you."

Reverend Eddie stood and walked to the door, his body filled with rage. He turned at the door. "Ray-Bob, you've been warned." He slammed the door so hard, the glass cracked.

Ray-Bob quickly opened it and called, "Eddie, you ever think of cutting 'em off, eunuch style? It worked for the monks!"

CHAPTER 24

(Pre-Murder, Rusty)

The public school system in America is normally divided into elementary, middle, and high school. Elementary is the beginning. As the name suggests, it's the most-basic first steps. Middle or junior high is a transition time, where kids become youth. It's a wild, wonderful time for all but their parents. Then comes high school, though where that name came from was anyone's guess.

When George Bernard Shaw wrote, *Youth is wasted on the young,* there were no cell phones or automobiles. An average American high school is a combination of sex and drugs, bullies and victims, jocks and nerds, scholars and nincompoops. Pleasant Valley High had it all.

PVH was small for a high school even by West Virginia standards. The physical plant facility was a flat-roofed sprawling one-story series of buildings similar in architecture to the women's prison elsewhere in the state. There were 278 students almost evenly divided by sex and grade for the four years of a senior high school, grades 9-12.

Rusty Bentley was a senior and within six months would be finished with his state-sponsored education. He could hardly wait to escape the hallways of doom. The floors were stained, polished concrete to resemble simulated granite. The walls were lined with lockers in long rows. Students congregated in twos and threes.

Larry Locke slid into the seat behind Rusty in their first-period World History class.

"Gettin' any?" Larry asked.

"Gettin' what?"

"That's what I thought. Your problem is you spell it H-O-O-P and put a basketball through it."

"You have no idea what it feels like to see a three-pointer separate that net."

"Spoken like a guy who isn't getting any." Larry smiled.

"I get my share. Girls like a guy with big balls, especially when they have Wilson written on them. You'd be surprised how easy it is after a game."

"I've seen you after a game. You leave it all on the floor. You don't even go to the dance, much less hook up with a girl. Rusty, I'm worried about you. There's more to life than basketball."

"I get my share," Rusty repeated, as the teacher began the class.

At sixteen, Rusty was already five feet eleven inches tall. Between his sophomore and junior year, he shot up five inches and was still growing, a skinny sapling without a trunk—all limbs. His arms were disproportionately long for his body, and his hands were perfect for palming the ball. That season, Valley was undefeated, thanks in large measure to Rusty's keen eye and his ability to fire a three-pointer with someone's hand in his face. He was shooting 50% from outside the circle, and college scouts were already watching him.

At the beginning of the school year, he broke up with his steady, Marge, who was tired of being second place to his practice. Rusty pledged to shoot three hundred times a day, every day, for 365 days a year. He pretended there were two guys against him, hands in his face, bumping his body, muscling him aside. He twisted and turned, as his legs lifted him into the air, then fell right or left as the ball left his hands. No matter what position his body was in while airborne, the hands always faced the basket, his fingertips kissing the ball when it left on its trajectory. He counted it as a semi-miss when it thunked through touching the rim. His shots must be net all the time, swishing with the science of kinetic sensitivity, feeling those three points before the ball left his fingers. He was at his best under pressure, as the clock ticked down, and his team trailed by two. When the ball swished through the net, it was a "Bentley."

Rusty's life was either basketball season or getting ready for basketball season. He practiced the year round. In the off season, he had enough time to have a somewhat normal life. Marge, a cheerleader, had been fun; but the relationship soured when he chose time with the ball court over her.

The beginning of the school year was trolling time, when members of the opposite sex sized up the new crop. Selections were made, then the fun began.

On the third day of the school year, Rusty saw a vision.

"Who's that girl?" he asked Josh Owens, his locker mate.

Josh looked up. "The new one from Beckley. I think her name's April O'Connell. They moved here last year."

"She's sort of hot."

"Yeah, if you like 'em plump.

"You need glasses. That isn't plump. It's ample."

April stopped at her locker, which was twenty feet from the gawking boys. As she opened her combination, she dropped a book. When she retrieved it, she showed her ampleness.

The drop was intentional. Basketball players weren't the only ones who practiced their moves. The image burned into Rusty's mind, staying with him the whole day.

The next morning, determined to meet her, he fiddled with his locker's combination until she walked past, then he waited for her to open her locker. He hoped for another dropped book, but she transferred her book bag and coat into the locker and took out a notebook and pen. She pushed the combination lock together just as he made his move.

"Hello," Rusty said. "You're new here."

"Sort of. I came here after the Christmas break last year."

"I'm Rusty Bentley." He offered his hand. "Where have you been hiding yourself?"

"I know you. I've been hiding in plain sight. I passed you in the hall a hundred times."

"I can't believe that."

She smiled. "You're Rusty, Randy Sue Bentley's brother, the basketball star."

"Player might be a better word. Yes, Randy's my sister, but don't judge me by her. I'm the nice one," he smiled.

"I'll tell her you said so. I sit beside her in Miss Oxley's English class."

"Don't believe anything she says about me. Remember, I'm the nice one."

April smiled and turned to walk away. On a whim, she turned back and held out her hand. "Good to meet you, Rusty."

He stepped forward and grasped her hand firmly like a politician running for the state senate. It was their first touch, and it radiated up her arm until her heart fluttered.

She blushed, stepped back, and hoped he didn't notice, which he didn't. He was dealing with his own reaction.

"See you later," he managed to mutter.

The bell rang, and he hurried off to political science.

It took the teacher going through roll call to break him out of his trance. "Here," he said, before his mind was back on April.

She's something else, he thought. *She's not snooty like the other girls.*

That evening, he cornered his sister, Randy. "Hey. There's a new girl, April something. She's in one of your classes, about your height, reddish hair, sharp. Know her?"

Randy met her only one day earlier, but Rusty's eagerness raised her hackles. "Yes. She's in my history class, then in the afternoon English class. Just met her yesterday, but I don't know. There's something about her. I can't put my finger on it."

Rusty's retort killed any chance of Randy liking April. "I'd love to put my finger on it."

"Crude. Is that all you think about?"

"Not entirely. Anyway, if she asks about me, tell her like it is, but don't brag too much," he said mischievously, but brotherly.

"Fat chance." Randy smiled leaving the room.

The next day after school, Rusty asked his sister, "What did that girl, April, have to say about me?"

She gave him a puzzled expression. "She didn't mention you."

"Impossible."

"Oh? You think all the girls have you on their minds? I think she's into that Gary Callaway guy."

"The skinny kid who runs track? Are you sure she didn't mention me?"

Randy was enjoying the conversation, but she had to meet a friend. "Not a peep."

Rusty realized he had some work to do.

The next day, Rusty was at his locker early and waited until April walked by.

"Hey, remember me?"

She smiled and nodded. He smiled back and walked off to class. He planned to have a little more interaction each day—a smile here, a joke or comment there, until the time came when he could walk her to class. She understood the plan and went along with it as a willing participant.

The morning before the third football game, Rusty decided to change tactics. "April, what about the game tomorrow night?"

"What about it?"

"You want to go?"

"With you?"

"Who else?"

"Sure, but just the game." She smiled. "I have a commitment afterward."

He felt pleased but confused. "You don't want to go to the dance?"

"It's not a matter of want to go. I can't. I have to be at a BYF party."

"What? I know what a BYOB party is, but what's a BYF?"

"Baptist Youth Fellowship. I'm one of the leaders, and I'm committed to go."

That wasn't what he had in mind, but he mentally shrugged. Going to a church party would be a first for him. "Fine, then we'll go to the game."

"Good. But will you want to go to the after-game party with me?"

"Honored. You've got a date." Where did those words come from? Oh, well, a church party, he knew, wouldn't be a make-out party, but it was a start.

Pleasant Valley High lost the football game, but Rusty and April had fun, and their classmates saw a new couple in attendance. They sat in the middle of the popular student section a few rows up from his sister, Randy, and her date.

When the game was over, April and Rusty walked the six blocks from the school stadium to the church. To his surprise, he had a good time. The other kids treated him with the honor of a potential all-state basketball star. On the way home, they walked past an open apple orchard and stepped among the trees for a kiss that was soft, sweet, and tingling.

He held her in his arms and whispered, "You're something else. I had a great time." He meant it, too.

She kissed him again. "Me, too."

One of the nice things about April was that her parents bought her a Jeep when she turned sixteen. It was five-years old, but it looked new and was as good off the road as on. Because of basketball between games and his practice, Rusty didn't have an after-school car. His father's policy was if he wanted a car, he had to pay for half of it and cover all the insurance, so Rusty walked.

The village was small; and, except in the extreme cold of the winter months, walking was tolerable. Occasionally on weekends, Rusty borrowed his mother's car for dates and weekend activities. Randy had a twelve-year-old Ford that was once her grandfather's car, but at least it ran well. She paid the insurance and upkeep with her part time job as a drugstore clerk.

April's car, along with her looks, was a real bonus. April, though, remained a bit of a mystery. Sometimes, she was distant and moody, as if she had two personalities.

CHAPTER 25

(Pre-Murder, Ohio River Day)

Indian summer arrived in Huntington in early October with a kiss of a heat wave, unseasonable but welcome after a cool September. Rusty and April stood on the banks of the Ohio looking at the sorriest boat he ever saw, a loaner from the assistant basketball coach at school.

The twenty-six-foot boat looked to be at least twenty-six years old and suffered from an extremely hard life. He wondered if it had any life left, particularly one more day. It was once white, but now it was gray, pink, and rust. Three of the four running lights worked, and the engine sounded like it was firing on five of the eight cylinders.

During recent weeks, he progressed from talking to April in the hall to walking her home, as well as their date at the games and at the Baptist Church. It was strange, but she was much friendlier at the church, as well as being a leader of the other kids. That was when she showed her best side, but it was still a very controlled event, with lots of older people in the background to make sure the kids behaved. Going on the boat would be the first time he would actually be alone with her, and he had hopes for the date.

The river was busy with other recreational boaters, as well as barge traffic. He was familiar with the Ohio River. His father had taken him and Randy boating and fishing often. April wanted more than easing along in the river. She wanted to water ski. What a surprise! She donned the set of skis secured against the inside edge of the boat and slipped into the role of a proficient water athlete. He drove the boat carefully as she performed flips and some other seemingly death-defying tricks. Who knew she could handle the rope that expertly? Maybe he could do that as well. When he saw how easily she did it, he felt it might not be that difficult after all. What could go wrong? The life vest would always keep him above water.

"April, that was spectacular! Even when the boat misfired, you didn't miss a beat. To be honest, this will be my first time, but I'm game."

"First time? You've lived near the Ohio all your life and never water-skied?"

"I'm more the fishing type."

She took over the controls, as he slipped his feet into the skis and prepared himself behind the boat with the line semi taut. The sudden acceleration and the sputter of the motor in a major belch of black smoke made the line tighten and then go slack and tighten again. Rusty was tossed around like a rag doll. He made the mistake of holding onto the rope after he fell, creating a wide spray of water, as April watched in amusement. So much for his wishful desire of being a talented water skier—the first time.

"Want to try again? Hopefully, the motor will cooperate this time."

"Sure. I guess when you fall, you should turn loose."

"Plan to fall again?"

"Give me a steady speed, and I'll give it a good run."

The boat finally cooperated, and, with his knees and elbows properly bent, he was waterskiing for the first time in his life. He was smart enough to let the boat do the work and concentrated on staying upright.

April made wide turns, trying to keep the boat steady. Finally, with a hiccup and puff of black smoke, the motor sputtered, and the neophyte fell. He released the rope and slid into the water as if he'd done it all his life.

"Wow. That was fun!" Swimming to the side of the boat, he pulled himself in.

A strange smell wafted through the air, cannabis mixed with gasoline vapor and fuel oil.

"Here. Want a toke?" April handed him the joint.

"Nope."

"Don't tell me that would be a first for you, too?"

"April, you have to understand that my father is the Chief of Police. Weed isn't on the menu."

"It's legal in some states. Sooner or later, it'll be legal here, too. It won't harm you. Come on."

He thought for a moment, then he took the joint and inhaled a lungful. The smell was already on him, and he would have to shower and sanitize his swim trunks before going home. He decided to find out about it, and he certainly did not want to seem too goody-goody to April. Neither of them put BYF in the picture at all.

To his surprise, there was no extraordinary sensation. Maybe he hadn't inhaled enough. He tried again with a deeper draw, then held his breath. His eyes watered, and he slowly walked away from April, pulling in air through his nose to dilute the potency.

Normally, breathing was automatic, but he was orchestrating the mechanics of the system. His body wanted to inhale, his mind countered with a violent exhalation by reflex, and he coughed hard enough to belch a cloud of marijuana into the wind.

Rusty, retreating to the aft of the boat, sat on the motor well. As April watched, Rusty almost went over the side when he fought to control his equilibrium.

He took a smaller puff and let it trickle to the back of his mouth and up his nasal passages for a quick circuit out his nose. He was content to sample the weed. It wasn't to respect or love it. He merely wanted to experience it and survive.

Within a few minutes, he felt comfortable with the experience. Smoke settled into his lungs and soon reached his bloodstream on its journey to his hippocampus. Rusty's arms felt hollow, and his nose tingled, as if he struck his funny bone. He laughed at the image of a crazy bone in his nose.

A few more puffs, and he needed to pee. Without caring they were traveling at fifteen knots per hour, he jumped overboard and released a warm urine flow into the cold Ohio.

April, laughing, stalled the motor when she stopped for him. When he pulled himself into the boat, he lay on the wooden seat to contemplate what he had done.

April tried to restart the engine, but it merely burped and groaned, as the starter made a whirling noise. "Rusty, did you check the gas when we got on?"

"No, but there is gas in the red can under the seat. Here. I'll pour it into the tank. The red can was partially full. Could the gas have moisture in it? The engine turned over, but refused to start.

Rusty steadied himself and flopped down on the only attached deck chair. "Let's give it a rest. It might be flooded."

The boat began drifting faster.

"I'll turn toward shore," he said. "Hopefully, we can float to the dock and not get turned out toward the current. Otherwise, we'll float to Ashland."

"Isn't that about ten miles downriver?" April's voice became fearful.

"Yeah. The only other thing we can do is try to direct her to shore. First, we need to turn around, then we have to break through the current to reach calmer water.

"April, you steer. I'll get in the water and try to pull the boat as I swim. With any luck, we'll reach the slower water closer to the bank."

On a hunch, he decided to try the motor one more time. Maybe it was just flooded and would work again. He turned the key, and the motor belched and hiccupped, but that was quickly followed by a roar. He adjusted the throttle, and the motor steadied.

Thankful, Rusty headed toward shore, oddly glad for the crisis that allowed him to show how he could handle a difficult situation. He didn't realize how uncontrollable April was.

Once they trailered the boat and were ready to head back to Pleasant Valley, April lit another joint.

"Rusty, you'd better drive. I'm mellow. Never felt so floating in my life. Come here." She wiggled a finger.

He, too, was enjoying feeling light-headed.

April opened the Jeep's back door and lay across the bench seat. "Could you please hold me for a second? I feel cold."

He climbed in beside her and closed the door.

His arms went around her, and she whispered into his ear, "I never felt so close to anyone in the world as I do to you this minute."

Her head was against his chest, and her small, sweet voice floated up to him. It was a new experience. He made out often enough with his old girlfriend and a few times after BYF with April, but this feeling was more intense, filled with urgency, almost an out-of-body experience. It spooked and thrilled him simultaneously. She raised her head to kiss him deeply.

"Rusty, I've never done this before, but I want you. It feels so right."

He was too far gone to quit, even though reason told him to slow down. A teenage boy with a hot girl in his arms seldom listens to reason. Worst of all, he was unprepared.

"April, I don't have a condom. Maybe we should wait."

"You don't need one. I'm a virgin. You can't get pregnant on the first time." He had never heard that before, but it sounded so logical and wonderful.

Soon, the Jeep windows were fogged from the steam of passion. April and Rusty merged into a harmonious blending that quickly reached the point of no return.

When it was over, they lay together for a moment, then he said, "Unbelievable, but we'd better get on the road."

On the way home, Rusty reminded himself to Google that new information about virginity.

CHAPTER 26

(Pre-Murder, Randy)

West Virginia weather changed quickly in the fall. A warm day could easily be followed by a chill from the Arctic, and everything would be covered by stiff, white frost. The air became thick and cold, and all living things left a ghostly trail as they passed.

The cold months looked good on Randy. Her knee-high leather boots met the bottom of her green A-line winter coat, which swished when she walked. Most people looked frumpy and layered, but she looked like something from the cover of *Vogue* in motion.

The walk from the school parking lot to the front entry was only twenty yards, but eyes followed her all the way. One male teacher in his late thirties turned to a colleague and asked, "Did we have girls like that in our high school?"

The other man laughed. "If we did, they sure didn't date me."

"Nor me." the first one sighed.

Randy Bentley was as smart as she was pretty. She was the Maypole around whom the Pleasant Valley High School danced. She was the social leader, and her brother the basketball star; but she was the one the other students most admired and emulated. For her, it came naturally.

She and Rusty were born four minutes and fourteen seconds apart. She was the older twin, the big sister, and, in many ways, the protector. They turned seventeen over the summer; and he grew four inches, while she grew only two. While he grew taller, she filled out from a girl to a woman. In physical and intellectual maturity, she was four years and fourteen days more advanced. His life centered on basketball. Hers was on education and friends. His friends were other basketball players and teammates. Randy's friends were everyone she met.

Her goal was to become a U.S. Senator. People gravitated toward her, and she reached out to embrace them.

For some reason, Randy and April didn't get along. They had two classes together, and their lockers were on the same wall within three feet of each other. Occasionally, they nodded to each other or said, "Hello," which was acknowledged with an equally anemic response. The lack of warmth may have been caused by Rusty's questions to his sister concerning April back when school started.

Randy simply did not like the way April was stringing her brother along.

Rusty and Randy had always been more than brother and sister. They were twins and best friends, something they shared since they were babies. Once they started high school, however, that changed. Randy no longer shared much of her daily life with her brother, and she definitely wasn't interested in basketball.

He accepted the change as a normal progression. Once he started dating April, a gulf appeared between the Bentley twins.

"You don't like her, do you?" he asked Randy.

"Not really. That's all I'll say."

"Oh, come on. There must be a reason."

"Just a girl thing."

As April and Rusty emerged as a new couple, the class lovebirds, Randy's opinion remained unchanged.

Rusty walked April to class. They met in the hall and hung on each other like dogs in heat. It was embarrassing for Randy, who was the aristocrat in school. Worse, while the two of them acted like white trash, April was also putting up posters for the church's anti-dance party. She became known as Miss A, which stood for alternative.

One large poster she put on the bulletin board read:

Alternative Party
Food—Fun—Games
Pleasant Valley Baptist
After Football until 11 p.m.

The local Baptists didn't believe anything good came from dance parties. They did not think it was a good idea for a teenage boy to put his hands on a teenage girl and gyrate his hips—worse, to hold her in his arms and press their bodies so close that a piece of paper wouldn't fit between. Dancing simply led to wrongful behavior.

Randy felt embarrassed that her brother became one of them. He traded his popularity and good standing to be Miss A's number-one fan. Her brother was a fool. Their romance heated up too fast. Something wasn't right.

Then, quite suddenly, April changed. Like a hot shower

Instantly turning cold, April became moody and unresponsive to his touch or voice. She told him she wanted to crawl into a hole and hide.

He tried to think what he did wrong. After considering many things, he decided none of them merited her sudden and weird reaction.

The fun of their relationship dissipated quickly. After the third day of her asking, "Why can't you be nice? Why don't you put me first? What's wrong with you?" Rusty began avoiding her.

The romance ended as quickly as it began. April walked to class alone, and Rusty was sullen, truculent, and reluctant to talk about it.

Randy was concerned and relieved, though she was sorry her brother was in such a funk. "Something happen between you and April?"

He didn't want to talk.

"Come on. What's eating you?"

"We just had a falling out. Besides, basketball is just around the corner, and I have better things to do than deal with a nut case."

Randy waited for more, but Rusty walked away. "Russ, you need to talk about it, just between us. It'll go nowhere. I promise."

"Nah. There's nothing to talk about. You know me. Climb the mountain to peek at the view, then head down the other side. I've got practice, and she wants to own me. I'm not ready. That damn church."

Randy couldn't help saying, "Sorry, but I don't know what you saw in her in the first place."

"You're a girl. There's a lot to see. It was a good run, but it's over. She has strange, weird ideas."

"That's why they call her Miss A."

"No." He gave a sad laugh. "Weirder than that."

"For example?"

"Not from me and not today. Someday in the distant future, maybe."

He walked away. Rusty, however, wasn't finished.

Two days after the breakup, Rusty received a text from April.

R I got to see u. must talk.

Where? When?

Big Bend 3:30.

Rusty was waiting when the Jeep arrived at the apex of Big Bend, a wide place just off the road beside the river, where vendors sold vegetables in season. That day, it was just a dusty brown spot with a few cellophane Heiner's Bakery bread wrappers and a white paper bag blowing in the wind.

"Hop in," April said.

He pulled himself into the passenger seat. "So?"

"So, I'm pregnant."

If she told him the world would end in an hour, it would've had less impact. One minute, he was a seventeen-year-old boy considering if he wanted to get back together with his girlfriend, and the next, he was breathless and spinning out of control, trying to stay in the moment and act like a man.

"Are you sure?"

"Yes, without question."

"You said it couldn't happen the first time."

"I guess I was wrong."

His fingers balled up until the nails dug into his palms. His arms tensed, and his breathing was labored. "April, I don't know what to say. I want to do what's right, but I'm not sure what that is."

She looked at him and slowly shook her head. "I won't get an abortion. I'm going to have the baby."

"That's not what I meant. I won't run away from this. I just want to consider the options. What do you want to do?"

"I need to tell my parents and then I need time to think. I'm not asking you to marry me. I just wanted you to know. Somehow, we'll work this out. My mother was four years older than I am when she became pregnant with me. And she was married. But I'm not sure that's right for us. There are so many questions and problems, including your dreams for basketball. I don't know where to turn."

A tear forming in her right eye slowly rolled down her cheek. He reached out to brush it away. He knew she was sincere, but, while she spoke about her mother, he considered what effect the situation would have on his upcoming basketball season.

When her chin sagged to her chest, and the tear rolled down her face, he felt ashamed.

His hand slid down to hold hers. "April, we're in this together. I won't run away. Everything will be fine."

"I hope you're right. I must tell Mom and Pat soon. I don't know how they'll react, but you're right. We'll make it through." She tried to smile. "I'll drop you off at home."

Neither spoke during the brief ride. As he got out of the Jeep in front of his house, he mumbled, "Good luck."

He watched the Jeep drive away, then he walked down the road toward a five-acre jungle of trees leading to a small creek. As he meandered through the trees, trying to collect himself, he found the large stump near the creek, which he nicknamed the Seat of Knowledge during better times. He sat down. He often went there, sitting and replaying games shot by shot, correcting the distance or the trajectory of errant shots. He watched water ricochet off rocks and slide over logs.

With his head in his hands, he wondered: *How could I have been so stupid?*

He opened his eyes to watch leaves bobble along, swirling in the current.

Finally, he walked toward home. He would wait to tell his parents. Maybe April was wrong. Maybe something would change overnight.

And change it did. The following day, Rusty received his first phone call from Reverend Foxx.

"Rusty, this is Pastor Foxx at the Baptist Church."

"Yes, Sir. What can I do for you?"

The voice on his cell phone was calm, each word precisely articulated. "I need to talk to you about April."

"What about her?"

"You know her condition and what you need to do about it."

"With all due respect, that's between April and me. I don't feel comfortable discussing it with you."

"Would you agree to meet with me and April?"

"I don't know. Let me think about it."

"Son, there isn't much time for that. The news will be all over town in a few days. You and April need to be a team and show you're in agreement."

"Reverend, I want to do the right thing, but that's for April and me to work out." He hung up.

Three days later, the school was aflutter with the rumor that Miss A was pregnant.

"She may not dance," one student said, "but apparently, she knows the horizontal mambo."

"Who's the father?"

"I think it's Rusty."

By 8:30 a.m., Barbara Chambers, one of Randy's inner circle, caught up with her in the hall on the way to first period.

"Did you hear that April O'Connell is pregnant?"

Randy's heart sank. "No, but I knew something was going on. People have been avoiding me in the hall. I hope it isn't Rusty's. I don't think he'd be that stupid."

"Obviously, a lot of people are saying it's his."

"I won't believe it until he tells me."

"I hope it isn't his. It would sure screw up his basketball season."

Randy flushed with anger. "It would screw up his life! That little tramp trapped him."

Randy went looking for April. After the first-period bell rang, though, April wasn't in her seat. She came in a moment later and slipped into the next seat over. Randy watched the clock for fifty minutes, her concentration on one thing. She ignored the teacher's discourse.

When class ended, she sprang for the door and caught up with April in the hall.

"April, I need to talk to you."

"I'm not sure that's a good idea. I guess you know." April kept walking.

"So, you're pregnant? Sorry." Randy said the last word simultaneously meaning it and not.

"Nothing to be sorry about. It happens. I'm not sorry."

"And you'll be keeping the baby?"

"Of course. It's mine."

"And the father?"

"Who do you think?" was the curt reply.

Randy, with all her debate training, knew almost any answer would be thrown back in her face. "I guess when you want to tell, you will. Anyway, good luck." She spoke smoothly and sounded sincere.

"Yeah. I'll let you know." April walked away down the hall.

CHAPTER 27

(Pre-Murder, Resignation)

The first church service on December 4, 2016, was packed. There was nothing like controversy to swell attendance. The choir finished its portion of the program, prayers were said, and the offering received. Reverend Eddie strode to the center of the raised stage and stood beside the pulpit, his left arm resting on it.

Slowly shaking his head, he began, "Church, we are in the last of times. All isn't right, even here in Pleasant Valley. There are rumors and stories. Let your ears be not deceived. We as a church, as Christians, will come out of this together, more firmly committed. Don't listen to gossip of the devil's lips. Individual members have situations that they, with the help of their faith and the Lord, will overcome. We must look to our own house and make sure it is in order."

His sermon was one of his best. Even his wife paid attention. From the pulpit, he read the eyes of his congregation, listened to the silence, and to the "Amens" that erupted spontaneously throughout his sermon. When he concluded and called for the invitation, he knew he was in charge.

The coming Tuesday night meeting with the Deacons would be delicate. He needed to announce Sandra's resignation at the beginning of the meeting. He hated talking to her about it, but he knew it was the only course of action.

"Sandra, can you step into my office for a minute?" he asked, passing her in the hall.

"Sure."

When she came in, he asked her to close the door behind her.

"Sandra, Tuesday night I have to see the Deacons for our monthly meeting. On the agenda is a letter from Jim accusing me of impropriety regarding his termination. This, in tandem with your divorce and seeing Ray-Bob, puts the church in a delicate position."

"Are you asking me to resign?"

"No. I'm asking you to do what you in your heart feel is right."

She'd known this request was coming, and she had prepared her thoughts. "I know that the pressure on you and the church must be huge when there's a member divorce in progress. I appreciate your letting me stay this long. I don't want to add to your burden any more than I already have. I know you tried to do the right thing; but obviously, Jim got the wrong idea. He's hurt and angry, and he focused on you as the man who wronged him. I tried to explain, but he won't listen to me. Tell them Friday will be my last day. I'm thinking of moving out of the community. I could find a job more easily in Huntington, and I can live with my sister for a while. Thanks again."

She was right. A burden was lifted, and the Deacons would have to trust him concerning his part in the situation. In a way, the meeting would be a vote of confidence in his ministry. Church secretaries came and went.

The other issue reference the BYF leader April O'Connell being with child probably wouldn't come up, especially if her stepfather Pat was at the meeting. Out of respect, the issue would be skirted, though Reverend Eddie knew it would come up if Pat were absent.

He had to bring that situation to a successful conclusion, too. Youth could be forgiven faster and easier than adults, especially if the young person confessed his or her sin and showed a desire to make it right. April needed to marry the young man as quickly as possible. Young love, even when misguided, was fine. Having an out-of-wedlock, bastard baby would take a while to get past. Baptists were improving in their tolerance and forgiveness, but there was yet a long way to go. Rusty had to do the right thing.

Later Friday evening, April wept violently when she told Reverend Eddie of her pregnancy. She wanted to speak with him first. She hadn't yet told her parents.

"It was my first time, and we were carried away. Rusty pressured me, but I said yes, so I'm to blame, too. I don't know how it happened. It wasn't anything I planned. I was saving myself for marriage." She looked directly into his eyes and lied.

He nodded slowly, completely unaware of the depth of April's deception.

Dear God,

It was with a heavy heart that I let Sandy go. It's for the best. I must put temptation out of reach. She's a beautiful woman, but it's too small a town. Besides, it's one thing to be tempted—even Jesus was. It's another to walk away. I did what was right.

My daughter, though, has been touched by the devil. Rusty Bentley had better do what's right, or I'll have to have a come-to-Jesus moment with him.

Both services had good numbers. I guess all is good or will be.

Eddie

Reverend Eddie did what he thought was appropriate and prudent. He recalled Matthew 26:41, *The spirit indeed is willing, but the flesh is weak.* He had his own internal battles; he was but a man, after all, and he knew it. He wanted badly to reach the top of the mountain, but his work was in the valley.

His immediate concern was April's condition. Mrs. Foxx had no idea April was Eddie's daughter. As far as he knew, that secret was known only to him and April's mother. He needed to get the Bentley boy to marry April quickly.

He considered praying about it; but it was his job, and he knew what to do. In a way, he was embarrassed to bring before God the problem of cleaning up his own personal shortcomings.

That Saturday night, normally a quiet part of Reverend Eddie's preparation for Sunday, he again called Rusty. That was his third call. He also texted him twice that day.

Seeing it was past seven, he called home. "Beverly, I have a lot on my plate tonight. It might be ten before I get home."

"Do you want me to bring over something for you to eat?"

"No. I'm fine. I'll try to wrap this up quickly."

Five hours later, he hung like a flag from the elm tree in the church's front parking lot.

The killing of the pastor was the talk of the town. The Mug and Plate added a third waitress to handle the crowd. Everyone wanted to catch up on the latest gossip, and a table at the Mug with three good friends gave people the opportunity to add their two-cents worth and hear the latest theory. Most people ruled out Beverly, though a small number believed she did it.

"Did you see her at the funeral?" the Safeway grocery manager asked. "Why, you couldn't even see her face. I'll bet she was hiding a big, fat smile."

His comment was greeted by a few laughs and a few moans from the crowd.

Sam Long, the village postman, took umbrage at the crude remarks about the widow. "You don't know her. She's a kind woman. Last Christmas, she gave me a card with a twenty-dollar tip. We need more people like her."

"So, you're saying a killer is a poor tipper?" Allan, the Über driver, asked. No one answered.

The leading candidate for the killer was Jim Spurlock, the former church custodian. After he was fired, he filed a complaint with the Deacon Board, saying Reverend Eddie had an unhealthy interest in his wife, Sandra. And, yes, a small percentage of people felt Sandra may have taken things into her own hands and killed the minister.

Second in the running was Ray-Bob, the barber. Everyone knew that the friction between him and the pastor was over Sandra, the church secretary. Perhaps both men had an unhealthy interest in the attractive woman.

"Women make you do crazy things," the Ace Hardware manager said.

Most men in earshot nodded in agreement, though a few did it mentally so no one would know.

"Not long ago," the Ace manager continued, "Reverend Eddie, rest his soul, slammed the barber shop door so hard that the glass cracked. Then Ray-Bob chased him into the street and shouted something like, 'Grow a pair.'"

"That could just be an argument," a man in the back said. "We all know Ray-Bob's a good barber and a little nuts in his opinions. There were times I wanted to slam his door as well, but try to find a five-dollar haircut in Huntington."

Kevin Bowen, an insurance agent, heard enough. "This was no random killing. Someone hated him. You don't cut off a man's fingers and hang him from a tree nearly naked unless you hate him and want to humiliate him. This was personal."

The plots discussed in the Mug could have scripted a soap opera for an entire season.

CHAPTER 28

(The Warrant)

The killing occurred on a Saturday night. The body was discovered Sunday morning, and the first letter from the Fist of God came on Tuesday. The funeral was on Friday.

The big break in the case also came on Friday late afternoon when the church's new janitorial crew came to clean up after the funeral. The crowd attending left quite a mess. It wasn't just the sanctuary, either. Litter spread over the entire grounds. The crew picked up an abundance of untidy remains of candy wrappers, baby diapers, plastic water bottles, Kleenex, etc.

But the most important item in the debris was a cell phone: Reverend Eddie's little black Apple. It had lost its charge and was as dead as its owner.

Scott Adkins answered the call when the cleaning crew reported the find. Needless to say, he was perplexed and amazed that such an important piece of evidence escaped his detailed crime scene examination.

On his way to the church to retrieve the phone, he wondered how he would tell the Chief about the discovery.

The cleaning crew member had picked up the phone and taken it into the church before calling the police station. When Scott arrived, he carefully retraced the man's steps.

"Thomas, please put the phone back exactly as you found it," Scott said. "Same altitude and attitude."

The young man was perplexed. "Excuse me? Altitude and attitude?"

Scott sighed. "You know. Put it back in the same place and position as you found it."

"Oh, sure." Thomas pushed the cell phone into a small crack between the concrete floor of the church's back stoop at the rear exit. He wore the plastic gloves Scott gave him.

A shiver went up Scott's back when he saw the phone jammed into the hole. He took out his own cell phone and snapped a picture of the barely visible iPhone in its hidey hole. Only a slight black edge was visible, and it looked like an irregular black rubber seam that separated the patio from the building. The picture wouldn't be useful in court, but it would save Scott a scolding from his Chief.

Scott placed the phone into a plastic evidence bag and set it on the passenger seat before driving back to the station. He considered various approaches for explaining the latest evidence to Bentley. He mulled over different ideas, realizing that sending the phone to the State Police Lab would take time.

On a whim, he headed for Wal-Mart on Route 60 and Nichols Drive just outside Milton. There, he bought an Apple charger for his car. Leaving the phone in the plastic bag, he carefully plugged in the charger and drove to the station, eagerly awaiting the phone's resurrection.

By the time he drove the twenty minutes to the station, the phone was working again. Bentley was at a continuing education class in Charleston, and Scott almost called him, but for what? The phone wasn't important, but the information it held might be critical to the case. Since he missed finding the phone in the beginning, he felt he had to redeem himself.

Redemption was important to Scott. In the eighth grade at West Junior High, he was accused of cheating. Unfortunately, he wasn't. He was just the middleman in the cheating scheme.

"Scott, what do you have there?" the teacher asked, looking up during the history test.

"I don't know," he said quickly.

The teacher marched to his desk and retrieved a small, folded piece of paper and read it.

1. Washington

2. Jefferson

3. John Hancock

"Scott, again, where did you get this?" she demanded.

"I don't know," he said, though he clearly recalled it coming from his left. It was pressed into his hand, and someone whispered, "Pass this on."

He didn't want to volunteer the information. He just accepted the note and was ready to pass it on when Mrs. Thacker saw him.

"Scott, this is serious," she said. "You're cheating. How did this get into your hand? Did it just appear spontaneously, like magic?" She knew who it came from and where it was headed, but she wanted him to say it.

"Spontaneously, yes, Ma'am. That's my best explanation."

"Scott, you're dismissed. Go to the principal's office and wait. You're getting an F on this test."

He failed the exam, but in the test of being an eighth-grade boy, he just got an A.

He had mixed emotions about the situation, and it followed him for the rest of his life. It was part of the reason he became a cop.

Eighteen years later, he was being tested again—to tell or not to tell? To protect others or to do the right thing? What was the right thing if it went against his personal feelings?

Sergeant Scott Adkins was short in an odd way. Sitting down, he appeared to be over six-feet tall, but when he stood, he was tall only from the waist up. He had short thighs, but his legs from the knee down were normal length. He couldn't wear Bermuda shorts. To add to it all, he wore size twelve shoes.

In his specially tailored police uniform, he was 5'4.5" inches tall, the shortest man in the Pleasant Valley Village Police Force. What he lacked in height, however, he made up for in attitude.

When he was a rookie, he was mostly on traffic detail. His height and baby face caused a lot of laughs and jokes. The citizens quickly learned not to ask if he were a Boy Scout when he pulled them over and knocked on their car windows.

Through attrition of more senior officers, Scott became the ranking officer under the Chief. Barboursville, a nearby larger village, and Huntington, the county seat, paid their officers appreciably more than Pleasant Valley, which meant the village police force functioned as a training ground for the nearby towns.

Adkins' problem was his final half an inch. He needed to be 5'5" to qualify for the other forces. Try as he might, stretching and sleeping with leg weights attached to his legs by a homemade pulley system, he couldn't gain any height. Police physical exams required the candidate to stand in his bare feet. By the end of five years in Pleasant Valley, Scott was second in command and knew that was the best he could ever get.

Chief Bentley was the third and most recent Chief he had served under, and he was taller than Scott by almost a foot. Bentley graduated from Marshall University, and had a Master's in Criminal Justice. He was overqualified for his job, and Scott knew the Chief would probably stay for only a couple of years to add to his résumé before moving to something bigger.

To say that Deputy Adkins had a Napoleonic complex was an over-simplification. He was better described as Napoleon's corporal. Chief Bentley bounced ideas off Scott. If he understood them, they were ready for dissemination.

When the Reverend's iPhone was charged enough to be useful, Scott saw that Reverend Eddie had called Rusty Bentley, the Chief's son, three times between eight o'clock and ten on the night he died. Even more damning was that Rusty called back at ten-thirty, half an hour before the murder.

Scott checked for recent texts and found the reverend's final message to Rusty.

> Rusty, I gave you enough time. I have tried to call you all evening. Meet me tonight at 10:00 at the church, or tomorrow I'll speak of it from the pulpit.

The coroner placed the time of death around 11:00 p.m., so Rusty may have been the last person to see the Reverend alive.

Then it hit him: Rusty could be the killer. The time was right, and there was apparently a conflict between the two.

What should he do? Scott realized he had to go against the code. He had to violate loyalty and forget friendship. He needed a search warrant for the Bentley home.

For a second, he contemplated calling the Chief, but he knew it was wrong to give the suspect's father advance notice that his house would be searched for a murder weapon.

He knew he should have called the Chief about finding the phone, and he certainly should not have recharged it and opened it without authority. It turned out part of that authority might be involved in a murder.

The Chief would be on his way back from Charleston and his mandatory training class. He would come to the office to prepare for the special meeting of the town council to update them on the progress—or lack of it—on the murder. Chief Bentley would expect to find Scott at his desk when he arrived.

Scott needed an hour to go to the courthouse in Huntington and obtain a search warrant. Then he needed to execute it, hopefully, without the Chief at home.

He came to a decision and called the Chief on his cell phone.

Chief Bentley had just left his obligatory class and had a Big Boy Steak sandwich halfway to his mouth when his phone rang. Seeing it was Scott, he debated whether he should finish his bite or let it go to message and see if it was important.

Instead, he set aside the sandwich and picked up the phone. "Bentley here."

"Chief, it's Scott."

"I know." He wondered why Scott always announced himself. Didn't he know about caller ID? He eyed his steak sandwich. "Yes, Scott? What can I do for you?"

"I just wanted to give you an update. I'm on my way to Huntington to get a warrant."

"Warrant?"

"Yes. We found a phone at the church. We think it belonged to Reverend Eddie."

"Great. Finally, a break."

"I'll be gone an hour or so."

"Fine. Keep me up-to-date."

Scott hung up, knowing he lied by omission. He told the truth, but not all of it.

His problem was getting a warrant. A judge or magistrate had to issue it, and the criteria required probable cause. He didn't have probable cause to search the Chief's house without revealing the information on the phone, but that created another conundrum, because he didn't have a search warrant for the phone, either.

Searching a cell phone without a warrant violated the owner's right to expectation of privacy, but how could a dead man expect privacy? Using the theory of the lesser of two evils, he sought a magistrate. The code allowed a warrant to be issued by an oath or affirmation before a magistrate or a judge.

A Justice of the Peace would be less likely to pursue the point of origin of the information. Scott decided to attack the matter directly.

Standing In front of the Justice of the Peace, he explained he was following a lead discovered while examining the deceased's cell phone. He showed the text and the timing of the calls just prior to the Reverend's death.

"This is about the minister's killing," Scott said. "We need it right now. We may finally have the killer."

The justice handed him a form labeled *Affidavit and Complaint for Search Warrant*. The two-page form had more blank spaces than directions. Scott scanned through it quickly.

> ...and that the affiant has cause to believe and does
> believe that property,

*a) (Stolen) (Embezzled) (Obtained by false pretenses)

*b) (Designed and intended for use) (which is and has been used) as a means of committing such criminal offense

*c) (Manufactured) (sold) (kept) (concealed) (possessed) (controlled) (designed and intended for use) (which is and has been used) in violation of the criminal laws of the state.

*d) (Evidence of a crime) Namely,

_____

_____

(State property to be seized)

_____

_____

_____

_____

Is concealed in

_____

_____

_____

_____

(Describe premises)

And that the facts for such belief are

_____

_____

_____

_____

(State facts for belief)

Below the terse language and blank lines was a place for Scott to sign as the Complainant and the fact that he was swearing to his statements and to the truth of the warrant request. At the very bottom was a signature line for the magistrate.

Scott drew a blank for the Chief's home address. He was there often, but he never paid attention to the address. It was the second white shingle-and-stone house on Tucker Street.

"Do you have a phone book?" he asked the justice.

"I haven't seen one of those since the turn of the century."

Scott couldn't call the Chief to ask. Most police officers kept their addresses secret from the general public. He couldn't go to the courthouse and search public records because the information would be officiated.

In a panic, he remembered the Chief bought one of the houses built by the Yeager family, maybe Robert Yeager. Within five minutes, he managed to locate the address.

In the place to describe the premises, he wrote, *714 Tucker Street, Pleasant Valley, West Virginia 26605 and its grounds.*

He swore the Justice to secrecy. "We can't let this get out. It's a big break in the case."

Bluffing and blundering, Scott finally secured a warrant to search Chief Bentley's home.

As he drove back to Pleasant Valley, he debated calling the Chief and decided against it. Normally, even with a search warrant, the police announced their intention of search to the home's owner, but this case was different because the owner was the Chief of Police.

He looked at the final signature, *William Jennings Huff, Magistrate.*

Scott's Crown Vic finally pulled into the driveway of 714 Tucker. He was relieved to see the Chief's car wasn't there. He got out, carefully checked his paperwork, and walked to the front door to knock politely. Randy Bentley answered.

"What are you doing here, Sergeant Scott?" she asked, using her nickname for him.

He tried to force a smile and rocked from foot to foot. "I'm looking for something pertaining to the Reverend's murder."

"Did you call my dad?" she asked, letting him inside.

"Yes, ah, and no. I talked to him about two hours ago and told him I was on my way to get a warrant. I haven't called him since."

"Want me to call him?"

"No. That's not necessary. I just need to look for some papers and things. You don't mind, do you?"

"No. Dad's office is the second room on the left down the hall."

Scott nodded as he walked down the hall. He wanted to search the entire house, but he would take one room at a time. As he entered the Chief's office, he felt strange. For a moment, he sat in the desk chair and looked at the papers scattered over the desk, with a computer sitting in the middle. Finally, he stood and went back to the living room.

"Randy, I have a search warrant. I'm sorry, but I need to search the whole house and the grounds."

"Why?" She looked at the papers, then grabbed her cell phone and called her father.

Chief Bentley was on his way back from Charleston when the call arrived. Randy explained the situation, and the Chief said, "Put Sergeant Adkins on the phone." He waited a second. "Scott, what the hell? What are you doing at my home? She says Rusty's name is on the papers."

"Sir," Scott stammered, "I...I'm here, because Rusty is a suspect in the Reverend's killing."

"No way. Not Rusty. This is a big mistake. Don't touch anything until I get there. Get out of the house and wait in the squad car. I'll be there in twenty minutes. That's an order."

"I can't do that. I'm here, and I have a lawful right to search. Chief, I'm sorry, but your order in this case is out of order. Please, think. I'm doing what I have to do."

The Chief's car accelerated to ninety miles an hour with his lights and sirens going. He felt sick. His heart raced, and he took gasping breaths. "Scott, listen to me. I'll be there within half an hour. I'll look at the papers. Please wait."

"Sir, you know I'd do anything for you, but I can't let you direct the search. There's too much of a conflict. I'm doing this to protect you, too. Sorry." He hung up.

Before he arrived at the house, Scott told Corporal Jenkins to find Rusty and keep him under surveillance. "Just watch him, but if he starts to get into a car or in any way leave the village area, detain him and call me."

Scott handed the phone back to Randy and went to the back door to look out. The Bentley's big yard sloped down a small hill in the back. At the bottom of the hill, a pond was more like a wide place in the stream flowing down the middle of the hollow.

As he stood on the back porch, he remembered the storage shed abutting the south wall of the house and walked out to it. The shed was locked. At the top of the door was a circular window. Seeing an Adirondack chair under a tree in the backyard, he lugged it to the door and stood on it, but he still wasn't tall enough to see through the window.

Positioning the chair sideways, he leaned it against the door to stand on the arm. The wood was barely a quarter-inch thick, but it flared over the brace. He stepped onto the arm and stretched upward for a quick peek. Inside, he saw a quiver of arrows leaning against a box.

Scott stepped down and kicked open the door. Directly in front of him was a Mountain Ozark Hunter Long Bow. He couldn't believe the size of it. It was damn near his own height, and it was heavy enough to require at least fifty pounds of pull. He took the bow and quiver to his car. The only other thing he needed was the family computer.

As he walked into the house again, he confronted Randy. "I need Rusty's computer."

"He doesn't have one."

"Sorry. Then I have to take the family computer. The only one I can see is in the Chief's office."

"That's Dad's," she said defensively. "We use our notebooks or the ones at school."

Scott, thinking for a moment, decided against taking the Chief's computer. With the weapon in his car, it was time to arrest Rusty. He thanked Randy and left her gazing after him, looking hurt.

But Scott also needed to leave before the Chief returned. Dreading the upcoming confrontation and Rusty's arrest, he went to his car and radioed Corporal Jenkins. "You have him in sight?"

"Yes. He's just wrapping up basketball practice."

"Let me know which door he comes out of.

Scott Adkins was waiting as Rusty left the gym and headed home. He pulled up beside Rusty as he walked down the road. Rolling down the window and leaning his head out, he assumed his professional voice and said, "Rusty? Over here. I need to talk to you."

Rusty came to the car. "Hey, Sergeant Scott. You gonna give me a ride home?"

Scott nodded and opened the passenger door. "Hop in."

Rusty pushed in his gym bag and some books as he folded himself into the seat. The car moved forward as the automatic door locks popped.

Sergeant Adkins drove silently for a minute until they were out of sight of the school and on a side street. He pulled over and parked.

"Rusty, we've got a problem."

"It's not Dad, is it?"

"No. He's fine. I need to ask you some questions, but before I do, I need to give you your rights."

"What? Sergeant Scott, I never did anything."

"I hope not, but I've got to do this. You have the right to remain silent...."

Rusty listened, not sure what to think. It had to be a prank.

Scott finished and asked, "Do you understand?"

"Not really. What's this all about?"

Scott took a deep breath. "The Reverend Edwin Foxx."

"I don't know anything about that!" Rusty shot back.

"Rusty, anything you say can and will be...."

"OK. I want to call my dad."

"You have the right to a phone call but only after I book you. Sorry. I have to follow the rules to the letter."

"If I can't call my dad, I want to call a lawyer."

"Are you invoking your right to a lawyer?"

"Yes, but I need to call my dad to get the lawyer."

"I understand. Once we're at the station, I'll let you call the Chief. In the meanwhile, since you've invoked your right to a lawyer, I won't ask you anything."

"Fine." He blew out a breath, leaning his head back against the head rest.

Instead of heading to the police station, Scott drove toward Route 60.

"Where are we going?" Rusty asked.

Scott shook his head. "I don't ask you questions, and you don't ask me. You should be in back wearing handcuffs. I'm doing everything possible to make this as easy as possible on you. I'm probably violating a dozen rules. Just wait. We're going to Huntington."

The rest of the trip passed in silence.

Rusty, pressing his head into the headrest, pulled his feet up to his chest in a near-fetal position. Every rotation of the tires, every bump, even the slightest jostle, was magnified through his body. He kept telling himself the situation was wrong.

Anger was replaced by incredulity. His only comfort was in assuming his father would take care of things.

It took forty-five minutes for the booking, mug shot, and incarceration into a holding cell. Rusty was then given his phone call.

CHAPTER 29

(The Chief)

Chief Bentley called Rusty's cell phone five times, but each went to voice mail. The boy must be at practice, and the phone was probably turned off and in his locker. The Chief was doing almost 100 miles per hour, racing past cars that pulled over to let him by.

He was ten miles past Milton on I-64 when he realized tears were running down his cheeks, which startled him sober. Slowing to eighty-five, he tried to control himself. "Oh, my poor Rusty."

Two miles out of town, he turned off the sirens and lights, not wanting to announce impending problems to the town. As he turned toward home, he called Rusty again without success. When he tried Scott, he didn't get an answer there either.

Randy was waiting. She already called her mother, who was visiting friends in Huntington. "Mom's on her way home."

He immediately realized he hadn't called his wife. He would deal with that mistake when he knew more about Rusty's whereabouts. He reached the porch and hugged his daughter.

"This is all a big mistake. I'll fire Scott as soon as I find him. Have you heard from your brother?"

"No," she said weakly. "He's at practice. I tried to call him."

"I did, too. His phone must be turned off. I'm going to the station. You tell Mom to call me when she gets here. Tell her I'm mad as hell but have it under control."

His next stop was the police station and its small holding cell. Corporal Jenkins winced when the Chief entered the building.

"Chief, Sergeant Adkins took Rusty to the police station in Huntington."

"Thanks. If Scott calls, tell him to call me. I must talk to him." Walking into his office, he flopped into the chair. His legs were hot and shaking, and his hand shook as he thumbed through his index for the Huntington Police Department number. Soon, he was on his way to confront Scott.

He kept trying to call Scott for that half hour, but Scott refused to answer for a long time. Finally, he did.

"Sir, I'm so sorry. I hope you spoke with Randy."

"I have. What's going on?"

"Chief, I wish I could discuss it with you, but I've been advised to treat you as hostile for your own protection. I took Rusty to the Cabell County Jail, so there would be no question of preferential treatment."

"Scott, you know he didn't do this. And you took him to Cabell County because you know I don't have a key to that jail."

"Yes, Sir, that among other things. Rusty's smart. He won't say a word until he sees a lawyer."

CHAPTER 30

(The Barber)

Ray-Bob's phone rang, as he was in the final trim of Anthony Hunter's hair. Tony was in his mid-eighties and had white, wispy, thinning hair. Ray-Bob had just combed it up to a point to trim when the phone played the first notes of the *1812 Overture*, which was Sandra's special ring.

She would have to wait. He wouldn't speak with her in front of Tony; and besides, the old man tipped well.

"Ray-Bob, you gonna get that?" Tony asked.

"Not now. Let me get you finished." He sliced through the little amount of hair.

The last few seconds of a haircut were critical, with the final touches, the comb-out, and the trimming of ear and nose hairs. Ray-Bob was an artist, and his signature wasn't on the final product until the cologne was gently applied with a slap of the face and he unfastened the paper neckband.

Ray-Bob pulled off the drape and shook loose hair away from the customer, much like a matador presenting his cape to a bull. The ritual of a haircut must never be rushed.

As Anthony handed him a ten-dollar bill, he asked, "You cut Reverend Eddie's hair, didn't you?"

"Yes. He was a longtime customer."

"I never thought I'd see the day that a Baptist minister would be killed and run up a tree in his underpants. Lord, what are we coming to? They still have no idea who did it."

Ray-Bob, mumbling something affirmative, glanced at his cell phone on the counter. As soon as the old man closed the door, he picked up the phone and called Sandra.

She answered on the second ring. "Have you heard the news? They arrested Rusty Bentley, the Chief's son, for the murder of Reverend Eddie!"

He almost dropped the phone.

CHAPTER 31

(The Chief and Son)

As the Chief's car neared Huntington City Jail, he received a call from Rusty.

"Dad, I didn't do it."

"I know you didn't. What made Sgt. Scott come after you?"

"Unfortunately, a lot of things...things I haven't told you. The preacher called and threatened me."

"Why would he do that?"

"I...I may have gotten the president of the Baptist Youth Fellowship pregnant."

"Oh, my God, Son. Don't say a word to anyone. I'll get you the best lawyer in town. In fact, don't say anything more to me. They might be taping this call. Understand? The only thing you should say is you want a lawyer, and you won't talk until you're represented. I'll see you within the hour. Hopefully, I'll have the lawyer with me."

He hung up and put his cell phone in his pocket before banging his head against the steering wheel. "This can't be happening," he muttered.

Needing a clear mind, he calmed himself and called 411 for information. "I need the number of the Pinkerton Law Group."

When he called the law office, he asked for Alan Pinkerton. "Mr. Pinkerton, I'm Chief Bentley of the Village of Pleasant Valley. About a year ago, we were on opposing sides in a law case involving a marijuana grower in our village."

"Sure, Chief. I remember you. I think you were a little hot when they dismissed the charges."

"Yes, I was, but I respected you and the way you handled that case. I have a personal problem and need your help. My son, Rusty, has been arrested for the murder of the Reverend Edwin Foxx."

"I'm so sorry. Where is he now?"

"The Huntington Police Department. One of my own officers arrested him and took him there."

"Can you be there in fifteen minutes?"

"Yes, Sir."

"See you at the booking sergeant's desk."

CHAPTER 32

(The TV Reporters)

Within an hour, the town was abuzz with the news. The WSAZ TV news truck parked in front of the Mug and Plate, soliciting interviews from patrons.

The long-legged, slightly plump woman reporter pushed the microphone toward George Lester, the local electric meter reader.

"What do you think of the fact that the son of the police Chief has been arrested in the murder of Reverend Edwin Foxx?"

The tall, skinny, fifty-year-old dressed in work overalls moved his gaze between the camera and the reporter. "I can't believe it. I don't see no boy writing *Fornikator* across anybody's forehead. I don't think young people even know what that means."

That wasn't what she hoped to hear, so she cut him off and looked for someone else. She was immediately sorry for her abrupt change. George was quickly interviewed by Channel 8, her competition.

CHAPTER 33

(The Acting Chief)

Arresting a suspect is the first step in a long, procedural-bound process of trial and punishment. Some say the trial is the start of the punishment. Public shame, incarceration, limited communication, and ugly orange jump suits are all part of the justice process.

While justice slowly moved forward, the rest of the village moved on. Chief Bentley hired Pinkerton, then he submitted his resignation to the Village Council.

They asked him to change it to an indefinite leave of absence. He wasn't sure he wanted to go back, but he took their advice for purposes of health insurance coverage.

Scott Adkins became acting Chief, appointed after Chief Bentley stepped aside. That wasn't how Scott envisioned becoming Chief. In doing his duty, he felt as if he betrayed his friend. Worse, he would have to testify against Rusty. He would explain the chain of evidence pointing toward the boy—the cell phone, messages, time frame, and motive. They added up nicely.

The valley police station was cold with bad vibes. The temperature could be regulated, but the mood and environment were negative. Scott's subordinates did not now joke or spend any time with him. He knew they weren't jealous, nor did they disrespect him. It stemmed from how he gained his promotion.

At first, he thought they'd adjust, but after four months, the chill remained as pervasive as a bad stink that refused to dissipate.

Nothing was more lonely looking than an overstuffed chair sitting by the curb awaiting a trip to the dump. Everyone experiences a similar feeling in life at some time, where he or she became the odd person out. Character would be demonstrated by what the person did next.

Weeks had passed since Scott talked to the former Chief. He missed his friend and felt bad that Rusty was in jail and facing a trial for murder. Scott knew he simply followed the clues that led to the Chief's son, but it still didn't feel right. The impending trial loomed heavily over Scott's thoughts. He would be the key witness who showed the path to a murder by pointing at Rusty.

The case would be heard in the Cabell County Courthouse with the Honorable Joseph H. Buchanan presiding. In his early fifties, Buchanan served as a prosecuting attorney before being elected to the bench. He was thin and fit from all the tennis, swimming, and back-road biking he enjoyed in the area.

Prior to jury selection, the judge, prosecutor, and defense counsel met in chambers to iron out the pre-trial motions. Even though all three men were within ten years of age and obviously lawyers, they didn't share the same mindset.

Some people are like corn on the cob, with their personalities on the outside, ready to emerge after a little foliage is shucked. Others are like lobsters, with a rocklike exoskeleton that is hard to penetrate.

Judge Buchanan was the toughest of the lobster type. He didn't believe in justice nor fairness. What was fair to one person was unfair to the next. He believed in the law, followed closely by procedure.

To him, order in the court didn't mean the gallery was quiet. People had to be quiet or be expelled. That phrase meant that due process would be followed. Procedure was paramount.

Justice was the product of procedure. Order meant following the law step-by-step. Seldom did he see one of his decisions reversed.

Often in open court, during a lawyer's eloquent argument, Judge Buchanan said, "Move it along. Come on."

No lawyer wanted to tangle with him. He didn't tolerate trivia or paratheatrical thought. In the middle of his desk, he had a plaque with a quote from Supreme Court Justice Joseph Story, who in 1829, said, "The law is a jealous mistress and requires a long and constant courtship. It is not to be won by trifling favors but by lavish homage."

For Judge Buchanan, homage to the law had a deeper meaning than honor or respect. He always followed the true meaning of the word, *to be vassal to the lord of the realm.* The law was his lord, and he served it.

The prosecutor and defense counsel both argued cases before the judge in other trials. Jack Daniels, the Cabell County Prosecutor, as well as Pinkerton, knew they needed to map their strategies based on the judge's peculiarities. It was a case where the referee influenced the game more than the opponent.

Prosecutor Jack Daniels stood 5'6" inches tall and had broad shoulders and a narrow waist. He was forty-four years old and a native of the area. His unusual name was easy to remember and a political asset. He first became aware of its oddity when he was six. He had just entered first grade at Johnston Elementary in Huntington when, a few blocks from the school, a large billboard announced *Jack Daniels Smooth!* Beside the words was a large bottle of whiskey. That was a revelation to Jack, who finally understood why people snickered when told his name.

A few days after seeing the sign, he asked his dad, "Why'd you name me after a whiskey?"

"Son, when your last name is Daniels, you have to have a Jack in the family."

Jack pondered that for a minute and decided he liked being special.

As a young lawyer, the name brought him clients. He maximized that advantage in politics with the campaign slogan, *This Jack Daniels is Strong, Smooth, and Sober!* It was a winning combination. The preacher's murder would be a watershed case in his career.

In early March, the three men met in the chambers of Judge Buchanan. It was a large room just off the main courtroom in the Cabell County Courthouse. The fourteen-foot ceilings were oak panels, stained in dark mahogany. Walls which had for years suffered flowered wallpaper were refurbished with smooth plaster painted a rich cream. The furniture was Spartan, but it was adequate.

The judge motioned the two men to sit. "Gentlemen, I know how you work. This case is a little different, and we must be careful not to let it get away from us. The press has sensationalized it. We have a preacher killed on church property, his bloody body hung from a tree; and, well, the picture in the paper with all the X's on it. We must proceed with professionalism.

"To complicate matters, the defendant is a seventeen year old high school senior and a local basketball hero. If that isn't enough, he's the son of the Chief of Police. We will proceed in an orderly fashion. We can't let circumstances control the curriculum."

Neither the prosecutor nor the defense replied.

"I have docketed the trial to begin three weeks from today. If that doesn't work for you, you must tell me right now and explain why."

Daniels looked at Pinkerton, then both looked at the judge and nodded acceptance.

"I expect all your evidence and lists of witnesses to be presented to this office by Friday."

"Your Honor," Pinkerton said, "there are many issues regarding the search warrant. I have prepared a memorandum outlining each. In summary, it was poorly written and executed upon a minor who had no authority to allow entry. The search and seizure of the bow and quiver of arrows was illegal."

"Whoa, my friend," Jack Daniels said, standing to emphasize his point. "The bow and arrow were on the property in plain view."

"Plain view, my ass. They were in a freestanding shed, not specified in the warrant. The shed didn't have an entrance from the house, thus it was a structure that could not be searched without a warrant."

Daniels smiled. "There was a window in the shed, and the deputy saw the bow and arrow in plain sight, thus he had the right to seize them."

"My learned friend stretches the truth. The shed's window is a round, decorative skylight over the door. The door is at least six feet from the ground, and the skylight is eight to twelve inches above that. Deputy Atkins is height-challenged."

"What?" Judge Buchanan exclaimed.

"Short," Daniels interjected.

"Yes," Pinkerton said. "Short. He's little more than 5'4" tall. To be in plain sight, he would have to stand on a chair."

Judge Buchanan raised both hands. "I'll stop you right there. I'll read your memorandum, but we must remember, this wasn't an ordinary search. This was a deputy searching his Chief's house. He was invited in by the Chief's daughter, who gave him permission to look."

"Just my point, Sir," Pinkerton said. "She's a minor and didn't have the authority to grant entry."

Judge Buchanan cleared his throat, giving Pinkerton a stern look. "Minor, spinor. It doesn't matter. She had parental permission to determine who she could invite into the home. Therefore, her age is irrelevant. Unless I come across compelling arguments in your papers, I will grant the fruits of the search, because it was not intrusive, egregious, or unreasonable. As far as the plain-view doctrine, Mr. Pinkerton, I will give you that one to take up with the appellate court. I believe if you review the inevitable discovery portion of the law, you'll set aside the shortness of the deputy. That may be a matter that will have to be taken up by a higher court." He smiled.

CHAPTER 34

(The Jury)

The jury pool consisted of members of Cabell County selected from voter registration records. Mr. Daniels had the first opportunity to question prospective jurors. The courtroom was almost empty, and a woman in her early forties walked to the witness chair beside the judge. Though it was an oversized brown wooden chair, it took the entire seat plus three inches of overlap on the left and right to contain her when she sat down. She had deep brown hair and a ruddy complexion.

The prosecutor approached the witness box where Ms. Shelia Garrett sat. "Ms. Garrett," he said, looking her squarely in the eyes, "Thank you for being here today. You have the privilege of going first. What do you think of that?" He waited.

"Someone had to. May as well be me."

"I will ask you some questions. This isn't a quiz. There are no right or wrong answers. Just tell me what you truly feel. Some of the questions may sound silly, but please humor me with an honest, quick answer. When you dream, do you dream in color or black and white?"

Shelia sat up a little straighter and looked around the courtroom, at the judge and the defense table. The question confused her. "I really don't know." She closed her eyes and thought. "Black and white. Yes, definitely black and white."

"Thank you. This next question may be harder. Please close your eyes again, if it helps. Do you see your mother or your father?"

"Father."

"Thank you." He turned to the clerk. "She's fine. I select her."

It was Pinkerton's turn. "My questions may be a little different from those of my learned colleague. What do you think of the prosecutor's questions? Were they cute, provocative, or unbelievable?"

"A little unbelievable. I thought he would ask about my background or what I believe."

Pinkerton smiled, bringing his hands together at chest height. "Thank you for your time." He looked at the judge and clerk and said, "Pass."

The next prospective witness was asked by the defense counsel to select a number between one and ten, then was asked his favorite color.

Ex-Chief Bentley was a little surprised by the jury selection method and asked Pinkerton about it during a break. "That was a weird way the prosecutor asked about colors, dreams, and numbers. Did you know he would do that?"

"Didn't for sure," Pinkerton replied, "but I've been in the courtroom with him many times, and he has a list of questions from some expert shrink, a Marshall University professor of psychology, made up for him. It's his secret weapon in jury selection. I had the advantage going second."

"What if he hadn't asked them that set of questions?"

"Then I would have, especially where I have a young high school hero on trial. I want a juror who picks a middle number other than five. I want a green or blue, no mango or fuchsia. I want a basic color except red and purple. Red and deep-color people tend to choose one or ten for their number. They're extremists who don't follow the pack or listen to logic."

"Why don't you like five?"

"Those are settlers, people who want to be safe, so they pick something in the middle where they don't have to think. Usually, they see their mother in their dreams and choose green as their color."

"I thought you liked green."

"I do, but not with five. Give me a green three, four, six, or seven who sees their father, and that's my juror."

"Interesting."

"It works," Pinkerton said. "That's all I can say."

For three days, the two lawyers continued their foreplay until a jury of twelve with three alternates had been selected. Both attorneys felt pleased with their selections.

CHAPTER 35

(The Trial Begins)

The trial began one hundred and sixteen days after the cherry picker brought down Reverend Eddie Foxx's body from the tree. R u s t y had been incarcerated for ninety-eight days in the Western Regional Jail in Barboursville, having been transferred there from Huntington since he was a juvenile. April was over one month into her second trimester as a mother-to-be.

The opening day of the trial, Randy was barred from the proceedings and was served to appear as a witness.

Rusty, wearing an open-necked shirt with blue Dockers and brown loafers sat between his defense attorney and Reba Sullivan, his co-counsel.

Pinkerton selected his attire. "No tie. I want a high-school look, casual but neat. We need to remind the jury that he's a kid."

Pinkerton and Daniels fought in the judge's chambers over handcuffs and shackles.

"This is a capital murder case," Daniels emphasized. "It's normal for the accused to be at least in cuffs."

"I totally disagree. It robs the defendant of his presumption of innocence. If the safety of the courtroom were in question, I would understand. I cite *State v. Brewster,* where the Appellate Court ruled that Brewster, a criminal defendant, had the right, absent some necessity relating to courtroom security or order, to be tried free of restraints."

Before the judge could comment, Daniels smiled broadly. "Your Honor, Brewster was up for robbery, not murder."

"Then I cite *State c. Linkous,* a first-degree murder case," Pinkerton said. "Again, the court strongly advised that in the absence of fear or immediate danger, the defendant should not be seen by the jury in shackles or restraints."

Judge Buchanan raised both hands. "In my courtroom, no shackles, no restraints, and no orange jumpsuit. We'll afford this young man his rights, every one of them."

He stood between the two lawyers like a referee in a boxing match, making sure each understood the rules of engagement. He knew they did. They had sparred many times before.

"Court will begin. Bring your best game."

A criminal trial is like an iceberg, with two-thirds of it hidden underwater. In a court case, it's hidden behind closed doors. Lawyers argue petty but pertinent points in the judge's chamber or with the legal counsel prompting or testing witnesses. The most-important consultation is the bond and communication between defendant and defender. Pinkerton was a master at eliciting the innermost thoughts and feelings of witnesses and defendants.

He was also an encyclopedia of legal precedents. They tumbled off his lips like a *Jeopardy* champion bettering his opponent. The one flaw or chink in his armor was a lack of empathy or understanding. He induced emotions from others but never showed his own. He was tightly wound. Like a fine watch, every tick or tock was accounted for and moved things forward. His passion was his work. He saw the defendant as a case, not a person. Personal emotions were for personal times, not while pursuing his avocation.

Standing for his opening statement, Jack Daniels stood straight, his eyes bright with a semi-serious expression that had a half-smile. "Good morning. We all know why we're here, but, for the record, this is a trial for murder. The defendant is Rusty Bentley, and the victim is deceased Reverend Edwin Ulysses Foxx, II. I know you're looking at this young man, dressed appropriately by his defense counsel, in a light-blue, open-collared shirt, slacks, and a nice pair of Cordovan loafers, telling yourself, 'He doesn't look like a killer. Even if he is, why is he being tried like an adult?'

"I agree he doesn't look like a killer. He looks like a high school kid. Ladies and Gentlemen, of the jury, he is both a high-school kid and a killer. Why are we treating him like an adult? Because of the horrendous method of the killing.

"The Reverend's body was strung up in a tree, nearly naked, and his fingers and thumbs were cut off so blood dripped down on the flowers below. What a horrible sight for the church members who found the body that Sunday morning. Rusty Bentley is being tried as an adult, so he won't return to our community with a mere hand slap by a juvenile court. This was a depraved act."

Prosecutor Daniels walked the narrow path between the jury box and the judge. He carefully made eye contact with each juror, being cautious not to stare with intimidation but to connect with their inner being, their feelings and intellect. His voice had the cadence of a preacher, soothing yet penetrating.

"We don't want this kind of killing in our community. We don't want this killer to ever walk our streets again. Over the course of this trial, the State will present evidence of hostility between the defendant and the victim. We'll show on the night of the murder, there were phone calls and texts between the two.

"We will further establish that the weapon used to kill Reverend Foxx was owned by Rusty Bentley. We have motive, the weapon, and the time frame."

He stopped, turned as if to walk back to his seat, then, almost over his shoulder, added, "Reverend Eddie was killed because he knew a secret about Rusty Bentley and was about to reveal it. We will prove motive."

He took his seat.

As soon as Daniels sat down, Pinkerton stood. (He relished opening statements.)

"You have just listened to the Wizard of Oz," he said. "He's standing behind a curtain made of doubt and misinformation. He ended with a clincher, a secret.

"There is no secret. The Reverend Edwin Foxx conjectured that Rusty Bentley impregnated a young woman who attended the Baptist Church. This was no secret. Half the students at Pleasant Valley High School thought the same thing. Look at that young man."

He stopped and waited for the jurors to turn their heads toward the defendant.

"He doesn't look like a killer because he is not a killer. If I asked Rusty to appear in a suit and tie, my esteemed opponent Prosecutor Daniels would have used that against him as well. We will show that the State has no case. There is no eyewitness, no DNA, no seeing-eye camera, nothing to tie the defendant to the killing. The best the State will show is that Reverend Eddie was pressuring the defendant. They will show no physical connection. At best, they will muddy the waters.

"I used the word conjecture a moment ago. Think about that word throughout this case. Conjecture means a theory without proof. That is their entire case."

As far as opening statements went, those were brief. The real trial would begin with the witness and the evidence. The prosecutor was first up. His job was to build the case and present evidence in an orderly manner. He was like a carpenter assigned to the morgue; he placed the nails in the coffin. Point by point, he would hammer home to the jury and judge the facts of the case.

His nails were timelines, phone records, murder weapon, and motive. He would not be equivocal. He would lay out his case precisely. Some of it would be circumstantial. It was his job to take the circumstances and reinvent them as facts or at least probabilities. His intellect and tongue were his tools.

His counter sat ten feet away: the defense counsel. It was the defense's job to bend the nails. Confusion and doubt were always on the defense's side. The two men were masters at their game, but it wasn't a game. It was as serious as anything could be.

The first witness to be called and sworn in was Robert Bentley. Prosecutor Daniels began his questioning.

"Were you, at the time of Rusty Bentley's arrest, the Chief of Police of Pleasant Valley, the town where the crime was committed?"

"Yes, I was. May I make a statement, a disclosure?"

The prosecutor stepped back, looking at the judge.

"Mr. Bentley," Judge Buchanan said, "you'll answer the questions as given to you by the prosecutor and the defense counsel. This isn't a forum. It's a trial, and you'll act accordingly."

Mr. Daniels continued. "Were you the arresting officer?"

"No. Sergeant Adkins was."

"Did you direct him to make the arrest?"

"No."

"In fact, it came as a complete surprise to you. Rusty wasn't even on your suspect list."

"That's right."

"You didn't even know Rusty was calling Reverend Eddie and threatening him."

"Objection!" Pinkerton said quickly. "A statement of fact that isn't in evidence."

"Sustained."

"Chief, did you know Rusty had been calling Reverend Eddie?"

"Objection! We just went over that."

"Your Honor, sidebar, please," Daniels said.

The two attorneys stood before the judge, discussing the phone records in hushed words.

"Your Honor," the prosecution began, "we have the phone records that show the defendant made two calls to Reverend Foxx, and Foxx made one to him on the night of the murder."

Pinkerton was livid. "This is wrong. We have a right to the evidence. They can't just come up with last-minute evidence and exclude the rights of the defendant. For heaven's sake, what happened to the right to a fair trial?

"Furthermore, how do they know the phone calls were threatening? Are they now going to say they have recordings? Are videos next?"

The judge waved the two feuding lawyers back and turned to the jury. "Ladies and Gentlemen of the jury, you will purge from your memory the statement by the prosecutor about phone calls. You'll take no inference of threats made by the defendant."

Pinkerton considered asking for a mistrial, but it was still early, and he believed in his jury selections.

The judge tapped his gavel lightly. "Mr. Daniels, you may continue."

"Chief, you weren't the arresting officer, as you stated. You had no clue that Rusty was the one who killed the preacher."

Pinkerton jumped to his feet. "Objection. Your Honor, that has yet to be proven. The defendant has pleaded innocent. The presumption of guilt must be proven beyond a reasonable doubt, not just made as a statement of fact by a loose-lipped prosecution."

"Objection sustained." He motioned both lawyers forward. "I'm telling both of you right now that this is my courtroom, and you'll respect it. You will also respect each other, as well as the law. This isn't a back-alley fight.

"Mr. Daniels, you'll stick to facts and the admitted evidence. Mr. Pinkerton, when you object, state a real reason, not an editorial comment. Understand?" He waved them back.

Mr. Daniels thought for a moment, deciding to change tactics. Addressing the Chief, he said, "You said at the beginning you wanted to make a statement. Let's clear the air. Make your statement."

The judge leaned over and said in a loud whisper that all heard, "Mr. Prosecutor, would you rephrase that in the form of a question?"

"Mr. Bentley, if you had the opportunity to make a statement, what would you say?"

Chief Bentley paused. "I'd say that I'm not here on my own accord. I think it unfair that the State of West Virginia has laws to protect testimony of married couples, that one spouse can't be forced to testify against the other; but there is no such protection of parent and child. I asked for a leave of absence, because my duty as a father is more important to me than my duty as Chief of Police.

"I had and still have no reason to suspect Rusty of this crime. I don't know what I can add as a witness, and I resent the implication that I was either incompetent or unwilling to do my duty in this case. The blood between father and son is stronger than an oath taken to uphold the law, but there was no conflict between me and doing my job. I understand there would appear to be such a conflict in the eyes of the law, so I asked for a leave of absence."

"Thank you. Now that we have that out of the way, I want you to look at Exhibits A and B."

Daniels held up two wooden arrows with shiny, sharp, triangular heads and differently colored feathers. "Do you recognize these?"

"Yes. They're arrows."

"Mr. Bentley, have you seen these before? Before you answer, let me introduce Exhibit C to the court." He reached to the prosecutor's table and pulled a small cloth cover off a quiver of arrows, handing it to the witness.

"This is Exhibit C. Have you seen these before?"

"Yes."

"Don't they belong to your son, Rusty?"

"No."

"They were retrieved from your house. If they aren't Rusty's, then to whom do they belong?"

"Me."

Daniels stepped back in amazement at the unexpected answer. "That'll make my next question a little easier. Look at the arrows of Exhibit A and B. Do they have the same markings as the arrows in your quiver?"

"Do you mean do they look alike? Yes. They're similar."

"Wouldn't you say they're identical, like twins?"

"No. I said similar."

The prosecutor let that rest, then he asked, "Did Rusty have access to your bow and quiver of arrows?"

"I haven't seen this quiver in five years. It was in the basement or attic or somewhere else. I forgot I had them. It has been that long. He never asked me for them, and I never saw him with them." He spoke in a calm, steady voice.

"No more questions."

Mr. Pinkerton stood, almost sat down, then stood again. "Chief, I mean Mr. Bentley, you collected those first two arrows, Exhibits A and B, at the crime scene, didn't you?"

"Yes. My officers did. I logged them in and turned them over to Mr. Daniels."

"Did you say to yourself, 'Boy, those look familiar?'"

"No, Sir. An arrow is an arrow. I knew they were hunting arrows, but they were totally unremarkable, just two arrows."

Pinkerton turned to the judge. "I have no further questions, but may we have a sidebar?"

The judge motioned the two lawyers to his bench again.

"OK, Mr. Pinkerton," the judge said. "What's your problem?"

"Your Honor, we have issues with the warrant obtained to search the Bentley property and the manner in which it was carried out."

"Mr. Pinkerton, we went over this in the pretrial. You know my feelings on this issue."

"Yes, Sir, but I've thought of it from a different angle."

Judge Buchanan took a deep breath and released it. "All right. Let's hear it."

"First of all, under the concept of *usa fruct,* fruit of the tree, the warrant to search Rusty's home was obtained on false pretenses. Sergeant Adkins used information found on Reverend Eddie's cell phone to obtain the warrant. However, he had no warrant to open the cell phone. It was a violation of the Fourth Amendment to the U.S. Constitution. There is an expectation of privacy, and this extends to a person's cell phone. Since there was no search warrant for the cell phone, and since the information on that phone was the root of the probable-cause basis of the search of the Bentley residence, then the whole search warrant should be thrown out.

"My second point is that the shed was searched, but it wasn't part of the warrant."

"Wait, Your Honor," Daniels said. "I'd like to address the first part about the right of privacy. Reverend Eddie's rights died when he did. His constitutional rights were gone at that time."

"I'm not asserting that the deceased preacher's rights were violated. I mean Rusty Bentley's rights. He had a right to privacy. This information was obtained without a warrant. Then a search of his house was conducted on a bogus warrant obtained with poisoned information."

The Judge eyed Pinkerton sternly. "That didn't fly three weeks ago, and it won't get off the ground today. I agree with the prosecutor. The Reverend's rights died when he did. As to the attribution of the defendant's Fourth Amendment rights being somehow violated, I find that a stretch.

"Obviously, the founding fathers didn't foresee cell phones and text messaging; but once it goes out to the nexus of electronic space, all expectation of privacy is abandoned by the sender. The pastor's cell phone could be searched by the sergeant, and the fruits of that search were legitimately and lawfully the basis for a valid warrant. Now step back, and let's get on with it."

The two lawyers returned to their tables.

Attorney Pinkerton had no more questions. Ex-Chief Bentley stepped down.

"My next witness is from the State Police lab in Morgantown. He's also a champion archer of Olympic caliber," Daniels said.

Captain Nelson was sworn in and raised a large, tanned hand. His skin was golden brown; and he looked like he lived outdoors, with his face wearing the railroad tracks of a captain in the West Virginia Wildlife and Forestry Division.

"Captain Nelson, I want you to examine Exhibits A and B. Have you looked at these arrows before today?" Daniels asked.

"Yes. Our lab weighed them, photographed them, and created a profile."

"How do you profile an arrow?"

"There are numerous ways of configuring an arrow. Shafts are normally aluminum, carbon fiber, or wood. These are wood. But, there are different types of wood. The most-common wood used in arrow making is Port Orford cedar. It stays true and normally gives longer life to the shaft. These are wood arrows, but they're southeastern Alaskan yellow cedar." He held up the white arrow for the jury to see.

"Looks white to me," Daniels said.

"It is. Yellow is part of the name. I guess it starts out yellow. It's good wood, but it tends to form high spots when it adjusts to moisture and environment."

"Why would a hunter or an archer want to use something that wasn't the best, that might run out of true or create an arrow that isn't straight?"

"Alaskan yellow is very popular with deer hunters, especially when matched with a Magnus snuffer."

"Wait a second. A Magnus what?"

"A Magnus snuffer arrowhead. It's a steel head with three blades designed to penetrate and stay true in flight."

"So, this arrow was designed to kill?"

"Objection," Pinkerton said, standing. "Leading and inflammatory."

"Sustained. Dial it back a little."

"Let me ask that in a different way," Daniels said. "If you were hunting a deer, would this arrow kill?

"Objection," Pinkerton said quickly. "May we have a side bar?"

The attorneys walked up to the judge's bench.

"Your Honor," Pinkerton said, "the prosecutor knows the arrow that killed the Reverend was a heart shot. He's trying to have his expert make this out to be a deadly weapon. He's giving it more weight than he should."

"No, Sir," Daniels said. "Not guilty. I just want to establish the profile of this particular arrow."

"Step back," Judge Buchanan said. "I'm ready to make a ruling on the objection."

The two men stepped back.

"Objection sustained," the judge said. "I won't allow the jury to be led astray nor be sensationalized. Counselor, please stick to the straight and arrow." He smiled at his own pun.

"Let's talk about the profile of this Magnus snuffer," Daniels said to the witness. "Can you explain the name?"

"Objection!" Pinkerton said.

"Overruled," the judge announced. "Continue."

The witness was puzzled. "I'm sorry. I'm lost. What was the question?"

"Please explain the name."

"Oh, yes. It probably came from the Norwegian King Magnus. He was known as the great one or the good one."

Daniels smiled, "So we have a good or great snuffer?"

The judge's bench reverberated, as he hit it with the gavel. "You made your point. Move on."

"Thank you, Your Honor. Let me direct your attention to the other end of the Magnus snuffer. Are these feathers unique?"

Captain Nelson slowly ran his finger over the feathers, holding the arrow so the jury could see it. "Yes, Sir. It's unique in that there are basically three materials for fletching or feathers. Cheap ones are made of plastic. Others are made of goose feathers and yet others turkey feathers. These are turkey."

"While you're at it, I see one of the fletching is a different color."

"Yes. That's the cock fletching. A hunter normally turns it up to minimize contact with the bow when the arrow is shot."

"So, it's traditional for three colors to be used, with the cock fletch being green?"

"Not necessarily. It depends on the manufacturer or a special order. Some people like bright colors or neon coloring, so it differs."

"Then a hunter might have many different arrows in his quiver?"

"Rarely. You buy them in lots, or you make them yourself. Personal preference dictates the style."

"Thank you. I don't want to put the jury to sleep, but I have one more question. What's this little section of the arrow called?" He pointed at the end.

"That's the nock, the guide for the string."

"Just a slit in the wood?"

"Hardly. There are some that light up when the arrow is sent. The nocks on these arrows are bone. They're custom cut or at least special ordered. Often, nocks are plastic. These arrows are unique."

"Thank you." He turned to Pinkerton and motioned him forward.

Pinkerton took the arrow from the witness. "Mind if I see it for a second?"

Captain Nelson handed it to him feathers first.

"Thank you. You say these are unique arrows. How many do you reckon there are like them? Fifteen, twenty, or more? A thousand more, or perhaps a hundred thousand?"

The witness looked at him.

"Excuse me," Pinkerton said. "That wasn't a rhetorical question. Could there be ten thousand manufactured like these?"

"I don't know."

"You're the expert. You know everything else. How many do you think there are? Five thousand? Ten thousand? Give me a number."

"Ten thousand maybe. I don't know."

"Thank you. No more questions."

The court recessed for the day.

CHAPTER 36

(The Confession of April)

The Barboursville law office was on the second floor of a white clapboard two-story house with a rusted tin roof. The driveway accommodated four cars. A jagged crack ran through the middle of the concrete slab. It is strange what is noticed when one is under stress.

Light rain, steady and cold, hit April's face, as she stepped from the car. The steps to the second-floor office were open to the elements, and she treaded lightly to ascend them. The door at the top led to a little hall that housed three small office suites. The middle one was identified as Mack W. Madison, Attorney at Law.

She didn't know whether to knock or go in. She pushed the door open and entered a tiny waiting room with a receptionist area cut into one wall. The receptionist/secretary was a plump woman in her early fifties in a sack dress that looked like it was from the early fifties.

She looked at April and asked, "Are you Mrs. Brown, the two o'clock appointment?"

"No. I don't have an appointment, but it's important that I see Mr. Madison."

"Have a seat. I'll see if he can squeeze you in." She walked into the inner office. "Mack, there's a young lady out here to see you. She says it's important, and she looks six months pregnant."

"Not guilty," Mack Madison said with a smile.

"You'd better not be. She looks all of sixteen."

"Show her in. Make sure this time to get her name."

She walked back out. "He'll see you. Who shall I say is calling?"

"April O'Connell."

"Pertaining to?"

"That's between me and the lawyer."

Carol Morgan smiled. This client would be interesting.

Mack stood when April walked into his office. He noticed her eyes were puffy. "May we get you a bottle of water?"

"That would be nice."

Mack asked Carol to get it for their guest. "I expect a client in fifteen minutes. I don't want to seem abrupt, but time is limited. How can I help you?"

April's lips were taut, and her cheeks quivered slightly, though she seemed to be in control. "Can we wait until after the secretary has come and gone? It's personal and private."

"I understand." Sitting back, he positioned his legal pad.

Carol came in with the water, then left.

"Now, April.... You don't mind if I call you April?"

"No, Mr. Madison. That would be fine."

"OK. What can I do for you?"

"I want to hire you. I have $800." Reaching into her purse, she took out a wad of crumpled bills, setting them on the desk.

He counted it mentally, but he didn't touch it. "Let's not talk money. First, tell me your problem. Why do you think you need an attorney?"

She pointed at her stomach and lightly tapped it. "Can they make me tell who the father is?" she blurted.

"Who are you afraid of?"

She reached into her purse and took out what appeared to be a letter, a writ to appear in court. She pushed it onto the desk beside the pile of money.

Mack reached for it. The back of his hand touched the money pile and moved it minutely closer. He studied the paper, ignoring his reading glasses on the desk. Although she was young and pregnant, vanity ran deep. He looked up toward the ceiling.

"You don't want to testify, because they'll ask you who the father is?" he asked.

"It's none of their business. Don't I have a right to privacy? It's my body, my baby."

"Yes, it is. One of our constitutional rights is the right to privacy, but a judge in a capital murder case has a lot of latitude. When constitutional rights collide, the judge rules which decision is the greater. He could, if he felt the paternity of the child was important to the case, make you reveal the name."

"No, he can't. I won't tell."

"He could put you in jail."

She burst into tears. Mack looked for a tissue but found none. He handed her a McDonald's napkin from a top drawer.

"Thank you." She dabbed her eyes. "That's why I wanted you to protect me."

"I can't guarantee results. You're a minor. There may be exceptions. I'd have to do some research."

"Then you'll take my case?"

"One more question. Why do you think the prosecutor in the Rusty Bentley case wants to question you?"

"Take my money first, please; and I will tell you."

"You have my word. I don't need the money. I need to know how deep you go into this."

She shoved the money across the desk at him. "I killed him."

His mouth dropped open, but he managed to steady himself. "You? You by yourself, or you and someone else put the minister up that tree?"

"No. I mean I caused it. The baby caused it."

Mack, still recovering from the shock, walked to the door and opened it. "Carol, cancel my afternoon appointments. I don't want to be disturbed." He closed the door without waiting for an answer.

"April, I want you to listen carefully. You killed no one. Causing something isn't a crime in most cases, unless you purposely intended your actions to start a chain of events that led to the crime. Think carefully before you answer me. Were you there when Reverend Eddie was killed?"

"No."

"Did you know he was going to be killed?"

"No."

"Then why do you think you or the baby caused it?"

"Because Rusty wouldn't have done it if he knew the truth. Rusty and I had a big fight over Reverend Eddie the night he died, and Rusty stormed out. He said, 'I'll get the bastard.' Then he slammed the door and left."

"Let's back up a bit. Why was Rusty upset with Reverend Eddie? What got him so upset?"

"It's a little complicated. The Reverend was calling Rusty, leaving messages on his cell. Rusty let it all go to voice mail. Half the time, he is practicing basketball and never answers the phone anyway. Then Reverend Eddie left a message about the baby. Maybe when Rusty heard it, he went ballistic."

"Did you hear the message?"

"Yes. Reverend Eddie told him to man up. That he couldn't father a child and then act as if it's just another notch on his belt. He said he wanted to talk. He told him I was desperate. He demanded Rusty call him immediately.

"Rusty was really mad that I talked to the preacher. He said, 'Something's wrong here. I'm not even sure it's my child. I want a paternity test.'

"I told him, 'Never.'

"He said, 'Just as I thought, you bitch.' That was when he stomped out and said he'd get the bastard."

Mack, setting aside his pen, drummed his fingers on the legal pad. "Do you mind telling me about your relationship with the Reverend?"

"He was kind and concerned. I thought he would cry when I said I was going to have a baby."

"And before that?"

"It started when we first moved here from Beckley. I was going through a tough time with my parents. I hadn't spoken to them in weeks. I said maybe a few words a day only when I had to. I was really mad. They took me from my friends and everything I knew. They did it to punish me, so I decided to punish them.

"One day in August, a few weeks before school would start, I was in my room and heard people talking downstairs. Pat, my stepfather, was at work, and I hadn't heard the doorbell ring. I thought maybe Mother had the TV on, but she never did that in the daytime.

"I decided to ignore it. If someone was down there, I wouldn't talk to them. After a few minutes, the voices stopped, and I heard footsteps in the hallway. Mother knocked on my door and said, 'April, you have a visitor.'

"I told her, 'Not today.'

"She persisted and said, 'This is important, Dear. Please open the door.'

"I was cornered and didn't feel like a big fight, so I opened the door and saw Mother and Reverend Eddie."

"Was that the first time you met the Reverend?"

"No. I saw him when I was dragged to church. However, it was the first time I saw him other than in the pulpit or shaking hands after church."

"What did you think?"

"My only thought was, *Oh, hell, do I have to put up with this shit?*"

"Then what happened?"

"Mother took my hand as a sign I should stop and listen, because it was something important, from the heart. I braced myself and waited. 'April, the Reverend wants to pray with us for better times.' Again, I thought, *Oh, shit.*

"Then Reverend Eddie took my hand. I was shocked by his firm grip and felt a strange sense of warmth. He squeezed my hand and asked God to bless me, to simplify my life and to protect me. The prayer was short and didn't preach at me. He ended it with, 'God, touch April and let her know she is loved.'

"That got to me, although I still thought it was hokey and was glad when they left. I sat in my room for fifteen or twenty minutes, then went downstairs. Mother was baking cookies, something she hadn't done in months and never in Pleasant Valley. I sat on a kitchen stool, watching and thinking how hard it was for her to go to the minister and tell him about our private, personal problems. My mother is reserved and very controlled. For her to seek help must have hurt her badly. I felt ashamed of myself and walked over to hug her.

"I told her my mute spells were over. I would try to adapt, though I couldn't promise I'd like it. I also said I'd try not to take it out on her and Pat."

"So that was your beginning with Reverend Eddie. Then what?"

"Church became a focal point. He was nice to me and asked me to be on the committee for youth services. One thing led to another, and soon, I was on the committee to help interview and select the new youth pastor. Reverend Eddie made me feel important and welcome."

"Was he ever inappropriate?"

Startled, she asked, "Do you mean, did he come on to me?"

"Yeah, or any other thing that was out of the ordinary."

"Absolutely not. We became close as in maybe a father figure other than my father." She looked away and collected her thoughts. "Nothing ever inappropriate."

"So, when you knew you were pregnant, you told him?"

"Not at first. I thought I might just be sick and missed my cycle. After seven weeks, I knew. I didn't know where to turn. I knew I'd start showing soon.

"One day, I went to his office and told him. I thought he would cry. He was trembling and couldn't talk. He seemed angry and confused. His first words were, 'How could you be so dumb?' That scared me. Then he apologized and said it must be God's will. He promised to be with me throughout. He also said I needed to tell my parents as soon as possible, although he advised me to leave his name out of it. He didn't want them to know I told him first."

"Did you think it was odd for a minister to ask you to lie?"

"No. I understood. He didn't want them to think I put him first. He did it out of kindness. He wasn't the kind of man who would lie."

Mack silently shook his head at her naïveté. "When did you tell him that Rusty was the father?"

"I didn't."

"Then why did he start calling Rusty?"

"I don't know. It could be because I brought Rusty to a few of the youth activities. Reverend Eddie once commented about Rusty being a fine basketball player, saying he was being considered for All State. He said that was a big honor for Pleasant Valley."

"After you told Reverend Eddie about being pregnant, did he ask about or mention Rusty in any way?"

"Never. That was why I was so shocked when Rusty told me about the calls."

Mack felt something was missing, as he continued his questioning. "You think Rusty read too much into your relationship with the Reverend?"

"Yes. He misunderstood. He lost his temper, and so did I. He pushed me hard to tell him why I went to the minister. I said I had to tell someone, because I kept it in until I felt ready to explode. He asked, 'Why not me?' I looked at him and wanted to tell him, but I held my tongue."

"You wanted to tell him what?"

April twisted in her chair, pressing her balled fist to her mouth. Finally, she cleared her throat and continued. "It was confusing. I didn't feel like myself. I was lost. I truly didn't know how Rusty would react. I lay in bed at night, sorting out the truth, praying, crying, thinking, and hoping I wouldn't wake up in the morning."

Mack stopped writing several minutes earlier, realizing he had a fragile, troubled, frightened minor in his office, someone who confessed to a murder she didn't commit. There would be problems in representing her without consulting her parents. He didn't know if he could shield her from confessing who the father was.

He doubted parts of her story. He watched her eyes closely, looking for deception, but he wasn't sure. A professor in law school once told him, "Just 'cause they say it don't make it true." The same professor demonstrated in a scripted mock trial that most witnesses tell only eighty percent of the truth. They don't lie outright, but they modify, adjust, and manipulate the truth, often unintentionally. It is a habit of self-preservation.

"April, you're my client, and I probably don't need permission from your parents, though I have to research that. Still, I think it's better they know about this. Have you told them about the summons?"

"No. I don't want to scare them."

Mack shook his head. Her parents definitely had to know. "How did they take the news about the baby?"

She lowered her head and stared at the floor, shaking slightly. "I haven't told them yet."

"Young Lady, you really don't want them to hear it from the witness stand."

"I realize that, but communicating with them is difficult. This is the hardest thing I've ever had to do."

He knew she was right. "Yes, but you have to tell them. Do it tonight. Do they have a drink or anything after dinner?"

"No. They're Baptist. At least, they are now. They would never drink in front of me."

"All I'm saying is, pick the moment and tell them both at the same time, so each one will try to protect you."

A little smile came to the corners of her mouth. She knew how to handle her parents and didn't need any lawyer's advice. What she dreaded were the follow-up questions: "Who's the father? When did it happen?"

Mack knew he faced a full afternoon of book reading and computer searches. "It will be for the better. Tell them! Get that out of the way; then we'll handle the court thing. I'll do some research. Make sure you let them know. Tell them you retained me. They can come here at one o'clock tomorrow when we meet for the pretrial conference. You and I will also need time alone to go over your testimony."

April was summoned to appear at the courthouse the following day at two o'clock.

"Meet me at one o'clock in Room 204," Mack said. "I'll reserve it. We need to go over how you should answer questions and prepare some hand signals in case you feel pressured, so I can object. You'll be fine."

Mack spent a long afternoon thinking about April and her story. She hadn't killed the Reverend, but she was far from innocent. It might turn out to be a lot of his time for a mere $800, but that was part of being a lawyer.

April was nervous, even after hiring a lawyer. Now someone else knew she was pregnant. She was scheduled to appear in court the following afternoon, but she knew she must go out of town to Huntington. Her parents, tomorrow's court hearing, nor eight hundred dollars paid to an attorney were not even considered. So much like April. Was it wisdom or stupidity of youth that directed her? There *was* Reverend Eddie's favorite verse that kept slipping in and among all the problems: *"For God so loved the world …"*

She hadn't seen Tim in over five months when she had managed to attend Marshall University's homecoming game with him. (Her mother, so impressed with April's BYF leadership role, had given her permission for what she believed was a shopping day at the mall.) After spending a wonderful time together at his apartment and then the pre-game bonfire, the fight started. She started it, and it ended in the proverbial, "I never want to see you again," shouted over her shoulder, as she ran to her car. She loved Tim and missed him so much. Why had she ruined their time together.

In the early days of her pregnancy, she felt bloated and out of sorts with everyone. Her mother and Pat just felt it was more of her rebellion. She began wearing longer shirts, sweaters, and jackets. She bought loose dress shirts that resembled tunics. At four months, she bought a Waterfall Cardigan that was loose and long, almost to her knees. Though she knew she looked pregnant, she soon learned people weren't very observant, especially adults, or they simply did not want to know. By now, many students knew, including Randy, Rusty's sister. Time was against her. Every day, she became more noticeable. It was time to leave town.

Sitting in her car in front of the lawyer's office, she punched in a text:

Tim Ferguson, do you love me?

April, oh, God, YES!

She read it with a tear in her eye and John 3:16 scrolling across her vision.

Meet at the mall in an hour. Starbucks.

What's going on? I've tried to call for months and was blocked.

Not the time to explain. Just be there.

I'll be there. He added a beating heart emoji.

CHAPTER 37

(The Bride & Groom)

One hour later, Tim was on the receiving end of a compelling argument for why they needed to go to Maryland that night. The two most important words April uttered were, "I'm pregnant."

He smiled. "That's great."

She put her hands over her face and began crying. "You meant it? You aren't mad?"

"No. I couldn't be happier. You're what I want."

April and Tim planned arrangements for their escape. She chose Maryland, because it was the closest state with the most liberal rules among the surrounding states for marriage age requirements. A doctor's certificate showing that the woman to be married was pregnant would allow her to marry at sixteen without her parents' consent.

True love at sixteen in the twenty-first century? It happened often enough for hundreds of years prior to cell phones. Why not now? Will their road be difficult? Most assuredly. Will their road be impossible? Well, that is their story to tell fifty years from now. *"Judge not ..."*

CHAPTER 38

(The Twin Sister)

The young woman walked slowly as she entered through the small swinging, half-sized door to the inner sanctum of the bar. The bailiff directed her to the witness stand.

Jack Daniels, in a dark-blue, pin-striped suit, stated in a loud voice, "Please state your name and your relationship to the defendant."

"Randy A. Bentley, sister."

"Aren't you, in fact, his twin sister?"

"Yes."

"A lot of twins think alike and complete each other's sentences."

"Objection." Pinkerton stood. "May we approach?"

Judge Buchanan, motioning them forward, asked Pinkerton, "What grounds?"

"Fifth Amendment."

"Did you flunk that section of law school?" Daniels asked with a perplexed expression.

"Mr. Prosecutor, I ask the questions," the judge said. "How is the Fifth Amendment relevant here?"

"It's where the prosecutor is headed with this. The defendant most likely won't testify, and he's protected by the Fifth. The prosecutor is trying to establish extra connections between twins, then he will treat Miss Bailey's answers as if they came from the defendant."

The judge considered for a moment. "I see your point, but I'll allow her testimony. There's no problem against siblings testifying. Tread lightly, Mr. Prosecutor."

He looked up and said more loudly, "Objection overruled. Continue."

"Miss Bentley, I just asked if you and Rusty, the defendant, have a special bond."

Randy looked at the defense table. Pinkerton nodded.

"Yes and no," she replied. "We're close, but we're very independent."

"Does he ever discuss his romantic pursuits with you?"

"Objection," Pinkerton said. "Relevancy?"

"Motive, Your Honor," Daniels replied.

"I'll allow it," Judge Buchanan said. "Continue."

"Miss Bailey, does Rusty discuss his girlfriends with you?"

"He has sometimes in the past, but sometimes not. More recently not."

"Miss Bentley, we're interested in the present or near present. Did Rusty Bentley have a date with April O'Connell within the past year?"

"Yes."

"Did he discuss it with you?"

"No."

"You said that quickly. He never discussed her?"

"The first day of school, he asked if I knew her. I told him she was in two of my classes. He asked if she said anything about meeting him, and I told him no."

"So that's the only time the two of you discussed her?"

Randy looked at the defense table and almost signaled for help, but she didn't. "He dated her a couple of months. We may have made a passing comment to each other about her."

"Did he tell you he got her pregnant?"

"Objection." Pinkerton approached the judge. "That's not a question. That's testifying. He's trying to put into the record that Rusty is the father, but there's no proof of that. This is subterfuge."

"It's a simple yes-or-no answer," Daniels countered.

The judge nodded. "Objection overruled. You may continue."

"Miss Bentley, did he tell you he got April O'Connor pregnant?"

"No, he did not."

Daniels stepped closer to the witness stand and turned his back to her, looking directly at the jury. "Then who told you Rusty was the father?"

"Objection." Pinkerton was already walking toward the bench, entering the well in front of the judge, reserved for the court clerk, and usually preceded by a request to enter.

The judge frowned.

"Facts not in evidence," Pinkerton said, stepping back to neutral ground, as Judge Buchanan robustly banged his gavel.

"Objection sustained." He turned to the jury. "Facts not in evidence does not mean there is no fact. It means there is no evidence so far produced that would support the statement. Therefore, you are to ignore the question. You are to draw no conclusion based on the statement. The prosecutor's question is stricken from the record. I rule it inflammatory and prejudicial. You will ignore the question and give it no weight in your consideration of this case."

Unfortunately, the jury members couldn't erase their memories. Just as a bell cannot be unrung or a motorist cannot slow down after seeing police lights in his rearview mirror, the jury now understood that Rusty was apparently the father and killed the preacher to shut him up.

The Judge motioned Daniels to continue his examination. Daniels wanted to do more damage, but he needed to tone down his approach a bit.

"Miss Bentley, did you ever see your brother shoot a bow and arrow?"

"Yes." She was determined to keep her answers short and to the point.

He reached over to pick up the quiver of arrows. "I draw your attention to these arrows. Do they look like the ones Rusty uses?"

"I...I don't know. I don't pay attention to that kind of stuff."

"But these could be his?"

Pinkerton was on his feet. "Asked and answered."

Randy didn't reply.

Daniels looked at the judge. "I'm finished with this witness but reserve the right to question again."

CHAPTER 39

(The Truth)

While the trial continued, Sergeant Adkins quietly slipped from the courtroom to follow up on a hunch. He drove to the AutoZone Parts Store on Route 60 in Barboursville. Despite the evidence trail, he just was not satisfied. His night was spent going over—yet once again—the people connected directly or indirectly with the main players of his case. His arrest of Rusty must not be a mistake. Acting Chief of Police must be honorably obtained. His friendship and gratitude toward Chief Bentley demanded it. If there is a remote chance …

"Do you have an orange signal lens for a front turn signal?" he asked the clerk.

"What year and make?" the clerk asked.

"Probably a 2010 Jeep Wrangler."

"They've got four on the front, two by the lights and one each on the sides of the fender."

"I just need the rectangular one on the front beside the headlights."

After he purchased the lens and carefully folded the receipt into his billfold for reimbursement, he left. Before opening the squad car door, he set the paper bag with the lens inside on the ground beside the car. He then stomped on the bag with his heel. Picking the bag up carefully, he took out the fractured lens, placing the jagged pieces into his coat pocket.

Fifteen minutes later, he was back in Pleasant Valley. He stopped in front of a small white house with a wraparound porch, walked up to the door, and knocked.

A minute later, Wanda O'Connell answered. "Well, Scott. Come on in. What can we do for you?"

"Oh, I don't need to come in. I just need to talk to Pat for a moment. It's Village business. Can he step out?"

She turned. "Pat? It's Sergeant Adkins."

Pat came onto the porch a moment later.

"Councilman," Adkins began, "I have a few questions to ask about the accident you had with the village police car a few months back."

"Took you long enough," he said.

Scott fumbled with the broken lens cap in his pocket. "If I remember right, you were pulling into a parking space at the Seven-Eleven when your left bumper hit the right rear bumper of the police car driven by Corporal Jenkins."

"Yes, Sir. He wasn't in it. In fact, he was just coming out of the store."

Scott pulled out the broken lens. "It wasn't your car, was it? It was the Jeep belonging to April."

"Yeah, that's right. We probably should've made a report, but the cop car had just a tap and a scratch on the bumper. April's car was the one with damage."

Scott leaned forward and stretched to his full height. "It's not so much the scratch, it's the turn signal lens on the Jeep that interests me. See, this is a piece of the lens from the parking lot at the Seven-Eleven. See this? It's a piece of the lens found at the Baptist Church the morning after the Reverend was killed." He showed them to Pat, pushing the two pieces together to show how they fit.

Patrick O'Connell's eyes followed the demonstration, then he looked down at the wooden planks of the porch floor. "It wasn't an accident. God told me to do it."

"Wait a minute. The fender bender or the killing?"

"Both. One followed the other."

"God told you to kill Reverend Eddie, then go run into a cop car."

"Of course not. He isn't crazy. I was coming back from killing that deceitful man when I remembered I had to stop at the convenience store to pick up eggs for Wanda. Just as I pulled in, Corporal Jenkins was coming out the door. I was afraid he'd see the busted light as well as blood splatters on my shirt. When the preacher's body was found, someone would put two and two together. I started to back out and leave, but we made eye contact.

"Then God told me to hit him. I was confused for a second, then I knew He wanted me to hit the cop car."

"Pat, stop talking. I need to give you your Miranda rights."

"God works in mysterious ways. I guess He now wants the world to know I eradicated that evil man."

Scott read him his rights from the little card he carried, ending with, "Do you understand?"

"I'd do it over again," Pat said, still rambling. "The only thing I was fearful of was that kid being on trial, but I knew God would protect him."

"Patrick O'Connell, I need you to turn around and put your hands behind your back," Scott said in a stern, careful voice.

"May I go inside and tell my wife I have to go to the station with you?"

"Pat, you're making this hard. I'll walk in with you without hand-cuffs, but make your explanation to Wanda brief. One step out of line, and you'd better remember I've got a gun."

"Thanks."

During the drive back to the village jail, Patrick wouldn't stop talking.

"I'd kill that guy again today. He was evil, parading as a preacher. I didn't go there to kill him. I just wanted to talk. He was having sex with my stepdaughter. She was only sixteen, and he got her pregnant.

"I was just going to talk to him, but then I saw the bow in the back of the Jeep and decided to shoot him in the ass. God wouldn't have anything to do with that. I missed the first shot and fired again, and the hand of God pushed the arrow aside.

"Then the Reverend saw me. He began running toward the car with his hands waving, saying, 'Pat, you don't understand. I'm so sorry about April. It was an accident. We didn't mean to do it. It just happened.'

"When he said that, I veered the car toward him, and the front fender hit his hip, throwing him down in the parking lot. It was a hard hit, too, like hitting a dog or deer. He jumped up and hobbled toward the bushes.

"God kept saying, 'Kill him! Kill him!' I jumped out of the car and ran after him. The bow was no good. I was too close. I grabbed him to pull him up and started punching him. He jabbed at me with the broken arrow. He must've picked it up when he sprawled on the parking lot.

"We fought, then I turned his hand back toward him and shoved as hard as I could. The arrow went straight in. He moaned and spat blood, then he gurgled, 'Why?' before he fell over. I swear God told me, 'Good job, Pat.'"

CHAPTER 40

(The Trial Interruption)

Acting Chief Adkins walked to the front of the courtroom slowly and deliberately. He tried to be inconspicuous and not disrupt the proceedings, but the Judge in his high seat followed every step the sergeant took with increasing irritation.

Scott bent over to whisper to the bailiff, "I have to talk to the Judge. It's urgent."

The bailiff turned to make eye contact with the Judge, who was staring at the two uniformed officers conferring in open court. Judge Buchanan stood, stopping the prosecutor in midsentence. "Excuse me, Mr. Daniels. We're taking a five-minute recess. You can return to your point then."

He banged his gavel once and walked toward his chambers, leaving everyone in the courtroom surprised.

"*In media res,*" Daniels muttered, walking toward the defense table. "Pinky, shouldn't we have been invited into his chambers? I'm not used to being stopped in midsentence by anyone but my wife."

Pinkerton, equally perplexed, but oddly feeling as if something good was coming for his defense. "We'll know soon enough."

Five minutes later, the bailiff ushered in the jury and said loudly, "All rise!"

The two lawyers exchanged a quick look, then focused their attention on the Judge.

"Members of the jury, you are not to read anything into this interruption," the judge said. "A legal issue was presented to me by the Acting Chief of Police of Pleasant Valley. After deep consideration, I have decided the issue should not be considered in this trial. It's a legal issue for another day and a different jury. Its validity or lack thereof is not your concern. You will purge from your minds any inference of guilt or innocence because of this interruption."

Pinkerton stood. "Your Honor, I call for a mistrial."

"Denied. I believe Mr. Daniels was articulating a point when we stopped."

"Your Honor, you can't just wave the interruption off as being irrelevant."

"I can, and I did. Any more discussion will find you in contempt of court."

Pinkerton, totally out of character, was red with fury. He felt as if his heart was in his throat, and his vision blurred as he considered the value of pushing the Judge. Reba, his co-counsel, reached foreword and tugged his suit sleeve.

"Whoa," she whispered. "Slow down. You've got this won."

Stepping back, he addressed the bench. "May we have a recess to consider the situation?"

"Granted."

Pinkerton turned to Reba. "Thank you." As he gathered his notes and prepared to visit the holding cell to confer with Rusty, the bailiff summoned him to the Judge's chamber. Daniels was already there.

"We waited," Daniels said with a smile.

The Judge motioned them to sit down. "Village Councilman Patrick O'Connell has confessed to the murder. However, that doesn't mean we abandon this trial. A confession doesn't necessarily mean guilt. Unfortunately, the councilman wasn't given his Miranda rights until he was three-quarters of the way through his confession. Also, some of his statements do not align with the evidence from the crime scene."

Daniels frowned. "What will you do?"

"I'm not sure. I was tempted to grant a mistrial, but I need to sort out this mess. I certainly don't want this information leaving this room. If the jury heard it, that would cause reasonable doubt. If the confession is proven false or tainted, I would have to dismiss them before they conferred on a verdict."

"So, what happens now?" Pinkerton asked, still in bewilderment at the news.

"First of all, I'll swear you two to secrecy upon penalty of losing your license to practice. I may continue the trial to conclusion. In the meantime, the jury is sequestered, and only the bailiff, the Acting Police Chief, and the three of us know this information. That's how it'll stay until I decide."

The two lawyers nodded slowly. The meeting ended like a prayer meeting, each person leaving in accordance but filled with doubt and confusion.

Within two hours, news of the confession was all over Huntington as well as Pleasant Valley.

Fortunately for everyone, another person came forward.

While Judge Buchanan caucused with the two lawyers, a short, fat man presented himself to the Pleasant Valley Police Department.

At first, the temporary receptionist dismissed him as a homeless bum when he kept demanding the see the Chief.

"Do you pay for information?" he kept asking.

He stood only 5'2" and looked as wide as he was tall. His sandy, dirty hair was pulled into a bun with a red bandanna wrapped around it. The white symbols on the cloth were a modified Confederate flag. He wore a dirty, gray t-shirt with sweat stains under his armpits and across his belly. His shorts were cut-off cargo pants with a wide belt that held a hammer, two sets of pliers, and a utility knife. Over his ankles were stretched white athletic socks over brown brogans. A faded red rag protruded from his back pocket.

"You pay, don't you? I got information."

"Wait here. I'll get the Chief."

Scott had just returned from the courthouse and feeling privately elated with the hunch development. The man standing before him, who was a couple of inches shorter than Scott, required another private elation. He offered the man a seat.

"You say your name is Johnson, and you have information?" Scott asked.

"Yes, about the preacher's murder. First, do you pay?"

Scott shook his head and gave a friendly chuckle. "No, Sir. No budget."

"Well, it's good information. It should be worth something."

"Doesn't work that way. In some cases, a reward for information is posed by the family or a third party. We don't pay for information. Can you imagine all the false leads we'd get if we started offering money?"

"Never thought of that. This is good. It's about the preacher killing."

Scott moved forward in his chair. "Tell me, Mr. Johnson, and I'll see what I can do for you."

The little man pursed his lips and shook his head. "Well, do your best. I think I saw part of the killing. Didn't know then it was a murder or crime. I just thought it was a fight."

"You were at the church that night?"

"Sort of. I was at the edge of the parking lot. I pulled in with the intention of taking a catnap. I had a couple beers at a tavern over on Route 10. As I drove on toward Hamlin, I felt a buzz in my nose, and my lips were cold. I remember thinking how the hell could two beers give me a buzz? I didn't want to get caught for DUI, so I pulled into the parking lot to sleep it off."

"Tell me what you saw."

"I saw two men. One of them jumped out of a Jeep-like vehicle and ran after the other. They struggled, and the man from the Jeep yelled, 'You fornicator you!' I hadn't heard that word in twenty years. I thought it was two drunks fighting over some woman. I left my lights off and backed out the way I came. When I was back on the street, I left."

Scott wished he had a tape recorder, but he also wondered if the guy was just another crazy he should shove out the door as fast as he could. "If you saw them, why'd it take five months to come forward?"

Johnson stared down at his feet. "Didn't know it was nothin'. I work behind Logan, up in the Dingess area. This killing might have been in the Logan paper, but I mostly read the funnies and the sports section. It wasn't until yesterday that I read about that basketball boy being on trial for murder. I put two and two together and knew it was the same church and the same night I was there.

"Well, Sir, it wasn't no skinny kid fighting with that other man. The guy who got out of the car was over six feet tall and athletically built, like a man who worked out or worked outside a lot. The other guy was a little shorter and husky."

Scott could barely keep his excitement in check. A bolt of electricity ran down his spine. Johnson's story corroborated the councilman's confession. This day could not get any better.

Scott had Mr. Johnson write out his experience on a legal pad and sign it. "Don't worry about the spelling or grammar. Just put down what you saw."

"You think you can pay for the information? I've got a job, and I work hard; but I've seen enough TV shows to know information is worth something."

"I wish I could promise. I'll see if there's a government program for helpful people like you. First, I need it all on paper with your signature."

Johnson began laboriously writing.

The following day, Judge Buchanan declared a mistrial without prejudice, *salvis iuribus*. That meant the current trial was over, but the charges could be reestablished if necessary. He was a cautious man.

Wanda, Patrick's wife, hired Mack Madison of Barboursville to be Pat's lawyer. He negotiated with the prosecutor's office a Kennedy defense, known in most other states as an Alford plea. It was similar to a no contest or *nolo contendere*.

Attorney Madison told Prosecutor Daniels, "Patrick O'Connell will admit guilt, but will affirm he isn't guilty because of uncontrollable rage that blinded him from being reasonable."

Daniels was reluctant. "A rage created by the belief that Reverend Eddie did what exactly?"

"To put it plainly, Patrick thought the Reverend was screwing his wife. Worse still, he thought the Reverend knocked up his stepdaughter. He was there to argue with the preacher, not kill him, but something made him snap."

"Let me get this straight, Mack. You want the councilman to plead guilty, but he's not really guilty, because he wasn't in his right mind? He's saying he did it, but it wasn't really him doing it?"

"Jack, you make it sound so damn crazy, and I guess you're right. It *was* crazy. His rage was uncontrollable. He was out of his mind."

"Then why'd he cut off the fingers? And where are the fingers? And where are the clothes? You do recall he was undressed up that tree? Looks like a cover-up, not an act of insanity. It's depraved, but he took time to hide evidence. What about that?"

"Glad you asked. He cut the fingers off after he returned to sanity. His rage was over, and he realized what he'd done. He couldn't bring the pastor back, but he understood that his DNA was under Eddie's fingernails. And, by the way, he fed those fingers to the fish in the Guyandotte River. The clothes are now ash after being fed to an asphalt recycler."

Daniels sat silently, shaking his head. "What a stretch! One moment, Patrick O'Connell is a raving lunatic. The next, he's sane enough to coolly separate ten digits from his victim's hands and plan how to destroy clothing."

"Jack, you have to separate the fingers and clothes from the crime."

"Well, Patrick certainly did."

Mack Madison chuckled. "If you take the case to court, I'll put Pat on the stand, and he'll tell the court and the jury how God told him to take an old bean can and saw off each finger. In fact, he'll add that God gave him to ten-thirty to finish the job."

Daniels knew putting a crazy man on trial could bring crazy results. "I don't know. I'll let you know tomorrow."

"Jack, I'm offering a guilty plea. You should've seen him when he found out Reverend Eddie was April's father; and Wanda wasn't having an affair with him. She was just trying to get help for "their" daughter. Patrick wept like a baby. He was in a rage, out of his mind when he killed Foxx. You might've done the same thing under those circumstances. I might have. Let us do the Kennedy thing and give him two years for manslaughter."

Daniels reflected on the young lawyer's eloquent defense. "Let me think about it. I'll get back to you this afternoon."

Mack Madison left feeling somewhat optimistic.

For the next hour, Daniels couldn't get the trial out of his mind. What a mess. It would be a field day for the media if he put on trial the church deacon who was also a village councilman. The longer the situation went on, the more likely some political opponent would stand in front of the Huntington Rotary Club and say, "Jack Daniels put a teenage basketball player on trial for killing that preacher. He must've spent $300,000 on the trial only to have to do another one for the real killer. That circus of two trials probably cost the county half a million dollars."

With that last thought, Daniels picked up his phone and called Madison. "Mack, tell you what. We'll make a deal and keep the fingers and clothes out of it. Five years."

"In Ona at the correctional prison?"

"OK. Yes, we can do that."

The murder was declared a crime of passion, a mistake of gigantic proportions on Patrick O'Connell's part. He was presented as a good man doing a bad thing. Even murder could get as little as five years in prison if someone had the right lawyer and the right circumstances. And most assuredly if there was a prosecutor who didn't want to be harassed by the press or challenged for his own mistakes in the pursuit of justice.

CHAPTER 41

(The Mug & Plate)

Justice might be blind, but the public is not. The killing of the Reverend Edwin Ulysses Foxx, II, was declared closed.

The Mug was elbow to elbow for weeks following the revelation that Patrick O'Connell was the killer. People stood in a sidewalk line out front to get in. Excitement comes unwillingly in times like these. No one can explain it. People are people. Something new, different, sad and terrible had attacked the community.

Ray-Bob had only forty-five minutes left on his lunch hour. Unfortunately, there was no other place to go.

"It'll be a fifteen-minute wait," the hostess said.

"Can't do that. By the time I order, and it gets to the table, I'll have to leave to get back to work."

"Would you mind sharing a table?" She pointed at a small table with one other person.

"I don't think so. I'll just order something to go."

As he waited for his menu, Ray-Bob glanced at the small table and saw the back of someone's head. He liked what he saw: luxurious brown hair lightly touching shoulders in a flirtatious way.

Oh, what the heck, he thought. "I'll share the table, if you don't mind," he told the waitress who came to take his order.

"No problem." She directed him to the booth. "Excuse me, ma'am. You indicated you'd share your table."

Ray-Bob saw the woman from the front and he was pleased with his decision and extended his hand. "Hello. I'm Ray-Bob. Thank you for sharing." He gave her a charming smile.

"My pleasure. My name's Edith."

Lunch soon became secondary to the chemistry between them. Neither said much before preliminary introductory remarks. They ate in relative silence, exchanging glances and smiles punctuated by chewing and swallowing. When one made eye contact, the other broke it quickly, as if it were forbidden.

Finally, it was time to head back to the barber shop. "Well, Edith, thank you for sharing." Ray-Bob reached for her check.

"Oh, you don't have to do that." Her hand touched his with gentle gratitude. "Unless I can return the favor?"

"It's a date. Tomorrow noon, here." He looked directly into her eyes.

"See you then." She smiled.

CHAPTER 42

(The New Beginning)

An old Murphy's law states: *The smallest hole will drain the largest tank, unless the hole was put there to drain it; then it will clog.*

Pleasant Valley was emotionally drained by the killing of Reverend Edwin Ulysses Foxx, II and the subsequent arrest and trial of Rusty Bentley. The Baptist Church was doubly hit. First, there was the murder of the pastor, and then came the arrest and conviction of one of the deacons.

Interim preachers took up the task of filling the pulpit for services. Soon, a search committee formed to find a new pastor. They wanted a man not too old or too young, preferably in his forties with experience and presence. Of course, he needed a good wife.

Jim and Sandra Spurlock moved to Huntington to separate apartments and continued their marriage by visitation.

The Bentley family sold their home, and Chief Bentley officially resigned. He took the position as Head of Security at Marshall University, where Rusty received a basketball scholarship even though he had missed the last nine games of the PVH basketball season.

Randy Bentley surprised her family and opted for West Virginia University in Morgantown for her Political Science major.

Scott Adkins was officially appointed Chief of Police of Pleasant Valley. (An anonymous donor left a new swivel chair at the station one night. It was low enough that the Chief's feet could touch the floor.)

Widow Foxx ran for the council seat vacated by Patrick O'Connell. She won, and rumor had it she would seek the Mayor's seat in the next election.

Ray-Bob Raymond and Edith Black were married in a civil ceremony at his Mud River cabin. A reception was held for them at the Mug and Plate.

April and Tim Ferguson had their baby and named him after his great grandfather, the coal baron. They never returned to Pleasant Valley.

Wanda (Emma) sought counseling and prayer to aid in her heartache. When her grandson was born, she held him with happiness, peace and joy.

How the young parents someday tell their son about two of his grandfathers will be left for the future. For certain, both were good men, believers and members of Pleasant Valley Baptist Church. And as Reverend Eddie preached many times and Pat O'Connell heard many times, "*For God so loved the world that He gave His only begotten Son, that whosoever believes in Him, shall not perish but have everlasting life.*" Sometimes it looks like the devil wins; but, then again, we hear Reverend Eddie's words proclaiming, "God always wins in the end."

As the Ohio River continues to flow and new days are brightened with dawn, Pleasant Valley begins the task of healing and once again becoming pleasant.